ALL THE PIECES

A LILLIE MEAD HISTORICAL MYSTERY

LISA ZUMPANO

FIELDING HOUSE PRESS

For those who bring us back.

THE LILLIE MEAD HISTORICAL MYSTERY SERIES

In Order

July 1923
Henley-Upon-Thames, England

1

"I see my dead friend."

A short glass of dark amber liquid was lifted to a pair of thin lips. A clink of ice. A swallow. "Usually, it happens when I am alone, but not always."

"Oh?" The man seated at the bar looked up at the clock, watched its steady tick for a moment and then reluctantly brought his eyes back to the person talking nonsense on his left.

"Yes. Often. Well, I'm on my own quite a bit, you see."

The man scratched at his beard. "As an apparition?" He raised his own glass and took a long, thirsty sip.

"Not quite, no." A sigh. "Mostly just pieces of her. Her nails, for example; they had little white flecks in them. Her eyes were the most magnificent hazel—with a deep green ring and dark lashes that curled naturally, they nearly met her eyebrows. They went perfectly with her hair. It was the colour of chocolate: dark, but not too dark. As though there was a bit of cinnamon mixed in."

"I see..."

"When she laughed I would laugh. It was as though she was

contagious—not her laugh, exactly, but her. Just her."

The man on the pub seat shifted uncomfortably. Who was this person speaking of dead people? One met the oddest clientele in the pub. No doubt the drink had quite a lot to do with it. He had just stopped in for a quick pint, mostly to avoid his wife. The later he went home, the less time he had to spend making conversation with her. But now he was stuck sitting next to this person—someone who appeared to have completely lost their mind. Someone seeing ghosts for Christ's sake. Or *pieces* of ghosts. His wife was beginning to seem more attractive. At least she was sane—most of the time.

The voice next to him continued, as though oblivious to the fact that he was a complete stranger. "But it was all such a long time ago now. Which, I suppose, is why it's so odd to see her as clear as ever. She must still be here."

Did he dare to ask? "How did she die?"

"Well, that's a bit of a story. As I said, it was some time ago now."

"I see." He didn't, of course, although he *was* getting more curious by the moment.

"Yes, she was killed through no fault of her own."

"How? Murdered?" he asked, gruesomely interested now. "Or an accident?"

"I'd prefer not to say."

How frustrating. "Of course, I understand. It must be very painful for you."

"It is. But I will say this. It's someone's fault and as sure as the day is long, they will be brought to justice."

"I hope so. For your sake—so you can find some peace."

"Thank you. However I'll never find peace. Not now."

The eyes beside him glinted steely and hard, the lips smiled thinly, giving him the strangest sensation of foreboding.

He shivered against the summer heat. It was time to go home to his wife.

SUPERINTENDENT FELIX PETTERS

The junior Henley-on-Thames police constable, a young man of twenty who had just recently joined the force, leaned forward over his knees and vomited. Petters gazed up and over him at the remnants of that day's festivities. Red, white and blue bunting littered the sky above a row of now empty banquet tables standing forlorn and abandoned. Devoid of their tea and punch, their parched tablecloths blew in the breeze—their crowds having moved on for the evening; house party after house party calling. Even the Thames looked done in: a swath of overheated murky green on a feverish evening.

Petters gave Jeremiah, his adopted son, a quick, reassuring pat on the back. "See if you can't go and find us something for dinner." It was an odd request in light of the scene before them.

The boy gave him a perplexed look with an accompanying eye roll, giving the constable to their left a scathing glance that spoke volumes about the boy's interpretation of the man's future career choice, but he yielded anyway and headed off in the direction of the abandoned tables.

Not that Petters was hungry after what they had just seen but it was a good excuse for the boy to be removed from the carnage in front of them. Watching his retreating back, Felix wondered fleetingly if Jeremiah's ability to be unmoved by violent death meant he might walk in his father's footsteps one day. But still, it was hardly a visual the boy needed to study and remember.

"Can you pull yourself together, constable?" Petters gently asked the pile of nausea before him.

The man nodded, wiping at his mouth with the back of his hand and straightening up. The Oxford University shell had been pulled up onto the grass before them, an eight oar model, beautifully varnished and now streaked in blood, its oblivious crew retired for the evening. Felix and Jeremiah had been cheering for them only a couple of hours ago from the second enclosure, watching as they put in a commendable performance culminating in a very respectable second place for their efforts.

But now this.

"When did the call from the stewards' office come in?" Petters asked, studying Jeremiah in the distance as the boy picked his way around the tables looking for any leftover pastries. Not that they should be eating anything that had been out in the sun that long, he thought with dissatisfaction. He felt his stomach growl its discontent.

"About six o'clock," the constable answered, tearing his eyes away from the racing boat and attempting to focus on Felix's face, his brow wet with perspiration. "Apparently they were undertaking a routine check of the boats before retiring for the evening when they found this."

He pointed to the severed head in the rear of the capsule—recently decapitated if the amount of wet blood was anything to go by. Male. Looked to be in his early thirties. Bloodied and matted blonde hair kept a tad too long. Two dead blue eyes stared back up at them.

"Have we any idea who he is?"

"No, sir." The constable spoke to Petters as though he were his commanding officer. Which he wasn't.

Felix and Jeremiah were on July holidays and had come to the Henley Royal Regatta as visitors. They had just had two sun-soaked days of fair-like fun and had planned to head back on the evening train to Oxford. This was hardly the epilogue he would have chosen to conclude their holiday.

"And the coroner? When can we expect him?"

"Any minute now, sir. He's on his way."

"Good." Felix scratched at his chin. "Well, I suppose you'd better start thinking about setting up a number of contingents to interview the teams. Starting with Oxford, obviously, since the body—or what's left of it—was found in their boat. We'll need to identify the poor fellow."

"Yes, sir."

"And get this area roped off immediately. I don't want anyone trampling over our crime scene." A slip of the tongue, *their* crime scene.

"What about the rest of him?" The wet-behind-the-ears junior constable asked hesitantly, as though finding a headless body now would completely do him in.

"Good question. We'll need to find it. Or your lot will. I haven't any authority here in Henley. Incidentally, where is your superior?" It surprised Felix that they would send a new officer to the scene of a murder.

"Probably at one of the parties, would be my guess."

Not very professional, Petters thought to himself. "You better find him, son."

The officer nodded.

"And find a crew to dredge the river, I wouldn't doubt that's where the rest of him is." Petters nodded to the head and the junior officer followed his gaze. "It isn't likely our killer would have dragged a headless body very far in daylight."

The poor man leaned forward and vomited again. Petters took a quick step back to avoid soiling his recently polished shoes.

3

HARRY

Orchard Cottage was bathed in an early morning sunlight. Its doors were thrown open to the advancing July breeze, and a whisper of grass and fading blossom blew through the airy, recently cleaned rooms. Behind the original cottage was a small new addition, a charming one-bedroom stand-alone home that was a near replica of the larger house. Although it had been built quickly early that spring, Harry had overseen the entire project himself. He had personally managed each stonemason, plumber, and carpenter. The decorator was inside now, putting the finishing touches to a pint-sized drawing room. A flash of pale straw fabric clouded the windows as Rumple attempted to hang a set of raw silk curtains.

Harry had hired a small army to get the cottage back into shape for Lillie's return to Oxford that afternoon. She had been in France writing her novel for the past six months and Harry had secretly feared every day that she would choose to go back to Manhattan instead of returning to Oxford. When he had last seen her, alone and cold on the train platform in the dead of an English winter, she had looked as lost as a lamb.

"They'll stain easily, you know," Primrose reprimanded, flicking her chin towards the new guest cottage curtains. "Silk is the absolute worst choice for anything other than a dress you intend to only wear once."

Harry frowned. "Do women only wear their dresses once? I daresay that would explain my mother's exorbitant clothing allowance. Last year it cost nearly as much as Father's Royal Ascot winner." He studied Rumple's exertions through the window. "I was trying to match the settee. My choices were limited. Have you actually ever tried to buy fabric in Oxford? Such paltry choices, the cloth shop is a veritable lion's den of hideous patterns and tepid wools. I told you we should have gone to London."

"We hardly had the time. I had no idea how all-encompassing this project would be. As it is, I am still astonished we've finished in time. Well, nearly anyway. What time is Lillie's train due to arrive?"

"Not until five o'clock. Thankfully. I want to have Nanny White installed and organized before they get here."

"Imagine," Primrose beamed, leaning into her husband. "A baby, here, with us. I'm so giddily excited to meet her."

The two of them stood at the threshold of the kitchen door and gazed about the garden. It too, hosted a beehive of activity. Harry had brought in the Tynesmore gardeners for the day and they were doing an admirable job of cutting the lawn and trimming the bushes. The sweet peas were in bloom and one forward-thinking trimmer had seen fit to clip an armload of them for the house. A pile of pink and white lay fragrant on the kitchen table awaiting their vases.

"I admit, I *am* surprised Lillie went off and adopted a baby girl. Just two months old -with her life? I suppose she will have to give up her job at the newspaper now. Imagine Jeremy Winston's disappointment. Poor sod has always been tragically in love with her." Harry chuckled his amusement.

"I don't see why she'll have to," Primrose answered, turning to attend to the flowers. "Isn't that why you've brought in Nanny White? To ensure baby Lola has consistent care. And I am infinitely available to help look after her. I should like nothing better."

Harry thought of the nursery they had also set up for Lola at Tynesmore in anticipation of helping look after her, and wondered for the hundredth time that day if he and Primrose would ever be able to fill their own nursery.

"It'll take a village, as the African proverb goes," he said softly, watching his wife from the doorway.

"Yes. And we are her village," Primrose tossed over her shoulder as she wandered into the pantry to fetch vases.

There was a knocking on the front door and Harry went back into the house through the kitchen to find a recently shaved and bathed Superintendent Felix Petters standing in the open doorway. Harry got a whiff of understated, earthy cologne. Not half bad, he thought.

"Good morning." Felix removed his hat and placed it on the bench inside the door. "What time are we expecting her back?"

"Not until five. Would you like to come for dinner tonight at Tynesmore? I'm hoping she'll be up to it. She's overnighted in London so I don't expect she will be all that tired."

"Good, yes, thank you. I've got something to speak with her about."

Harry raised a dark-blonde eyebrow. The man could be impossibly cryptic. "Murder? Mayhem? Vicar's lost his resident owl? The man can be so exhaustingly eccentric."

"Something like that," Petters said, glancing around the room. "Quite a bustle of activity around here."

"Mm. Yes. Rather like a wedding, I suppose. Or possibly a wake. And apparently the dismal new curtains I've chosen are disposable," Harry lamented, attempting to look at everything through his visitor's eyes.

"I don't suppose you know anyone on the Oxford rowing team, do you?" Petters asked.

"This year's team? I heard they put in an admirable performance at Henley."

"Second place. Yes," Petters confirmed.

"I suppose they wanted the gold, though. They always do. But in answer to your question, I do know the coxswain, Will Andrews. Friendly enough fellow. Been there for a few years anyway, mostly because the poor chap can't seem to actually finish his schooling. I do rather think he might never leave. One will likely find him pressed in the stacks of the Bodleian Library fifty years from now, preserved in an over-sized replica of the Magna Carta, reeking of parchment and iron-gall ink. Can't say I'm too familiar with the rest of the crew though. Why do you ask?"

"There was a bit of an incident in Henley yesterday."

"What sort of an incident? Overturned boat manned by a team of drunkards from Cambridge?"

"Not quite. But it's nothing I should speak of now—I can fill you in later this evening, along with Lillie."

Harry gave this some thought and chose his words carefully. "She's a mother now, Felix. I don't suppose she will be the same Lillie who left Oxford six months ago." It was a warning, certainly, but a gentle one.

Petters nodded his understanding, but didn't look as though he agreed. Either way they would see when her train arrived.

For Harry, at least, it nearly felt like Christmas morning.

4

LILLIE

The train wound its way through the Oxfordshire countryside, a great hulking black snake steaming its way home. The heat of the day beat through the carriage windows, and those that were open offered little respite to an unusually warm English summer.

Lillie loosened the little bundle of ivory blankets on her lap. She placed a hand on the baby's stomach and curled another around her body, hugging her close while Lola slept. She had the strangest sensation that she assumed every new mother had when they looked at their child—that they would quite easily kill anyone or anything that came between them.

The incessant rocking of the train was the perfect antidote to a sleepless London night. The rest of the train compartment was comparatively empty with the exception of an old woman who shifted her body now and then in order to accommodate her arthritic joints. She had told Lillie all about her ailments on the first leg of the journey and Lillie had patiently listened while jiggling a discontented Lola to sleep and trying to give the woman the attention she so obviously craved.

Now was the first time she'd had any quiet, and it gave her

time to prepare for their arrival in Oxford. She knew Harry and Primrose would be there to greet her and she was ridiculously excited to see them. She thought briefly of Jack. The last time she had seen him had been just before she left for Provence. He had written a couple of times while she had been away, and she had written in return, mostly keeping the discussion to the landscape where she resided. A small farmhouse on the outskirts of Aix nestled among fields of lavender as far as the eye could see. She spoke to him of her novel, and he of what little he could say of his work, and their superficial correspondence allowed her to be content with their new friendship.

Falling out of love with someone took time, but for her at least, when the curtains came down it was the final end of the performance. She didn't do encores. Jack had returned to London after her departure, so he had said, and hadn't been in Oxford since. Camille, the woman he'd had relations with during the war, and their son Adrien had also left for London and although he didn't speak of them, Lillie assumed they had begun their life together, the three of them. It no longer tugged at her heart, for that was the thing about getting over someone: they no longer had the power to affect you. It was the most freeing thing, to leave behind something that no longer made you happy.

Lola stirred, making a sucking sound and reached up with one tiny hand, eyes closed. Lillie watched as the bundle of life before her chose sleep over wakefulness and settled back into a peaceful slumber. They were only a few minutes out. A few minutes until she saw Harry and Primrose. She gingerly leaned over and started to gather their things together. The old woman across from them was fast asleep now, her breath coming in short, sharp blasts. Lillie yawned, wishing for sleep herself. But there was plenty of time for that—first, *home*.

By the time Oxford Station loomed large outside her window, the train sounding its whistle across a content afternoon, Lillie was wide awake. She said her goodbyes to the old woman and carefully made her way from the train with sleeping Lola cradled in her arms. A young porter followed behind with her bags. She saw Harry before he saw her, his flaxen hair pushed back, his eyes searching the crowd of travellers and greeters. Beside him was the glossy dark hair of Primrose. Lillie raised a hand and gave them a wave to which Primrose gave a nearly hysterical cry.

"She's here! Lillie! Harry..." Prim rushed forward nearly toppling those in her way. "Ohhhh, look at this little beauty." She reached out her arms to Lola and Lillie carefully deposited the sleeping bundle into them. Prim's eyes immediately filled as she gazed down at the baby.

"Meet Lola, Oxford's newest addition." Lillie smiled. "I can't tell you how happy I am to see you both." She gave Primrose a kiss on the cheek, noting that her friend's attention was entirely on baby Lola and for the moment at least, it was as though she didn't exist. Which was perfectly as the world should be when there was a new life in it.

Harry stepped forward, oddly speechless, and embraced her in an enormous hug. "Don't *ever* go away again," he said quietly into her hair. "I mean it. I thought you would never return."

Lillie hugged him back for all she was worth. Friends, she reflected, were forever. Behind Harry, standing alert and apart was Rumple, Harry's manservant, clothed impeccably in a chauffeur's uniform that looked as though it was possibly Indian in origin—it was fitting given the summer they were having, if faintly ridiculous. Having traded the traditional heavy English wool for the white trousers and short-sleeved shirt he wore now, he would have been quite at home in Bombay. He had removed his cap and twisted it in his hands while he peered forward to get a look at Lola.

"Rumple." Lillie extracted herself from Harry and shook his hand. "I've missed you."

"Miss Mead. Welcome home. Oxford hasn't been the same without you." He grasped her hand. "And I see you have brought us someone special."

"Well," Harry announced over the din of the disembarking crowd. "Shall we?" He motioned to the exit and the five of them, followed by the porter, made their way to Harry's impeccably polished awaiting Rolls Royce.

Oxford had never looked so good.

5

The back door was left wide open, pried open as it was —the lock splintered and lying in pieces on the cobblestones. The heavy scent of grease and fried onions spilled into the alleyway. She was there with them, her rounded fingertips, their flecks of white under the nails, those clear hazel eyes smiling at the scene before them. And then the two of them laughed, as they used to. As if they were still together. Their hired help looked at them as though they were mad.

The evening was hot, hotter than it had been in some time in England, and sweat poured down their skin. Even she was sweating, or so it seemed, which in itself didn't seem at all odd unless one stopped to really think about it.

They had dragged their target out of the restaurant after its closing. They knew enough from surveilling him that he would be the only employee left at this hour. He was unconscious now —owing chiefly to the blow they had administered, causing him to slip on his recently mopped kitchen floor and crumple to the ground—and they heaved his body into the back of the small car, shoving and pushing until they could manage to get the door closed. His left shoe fell off in the process and they didn't even bother to retrieve it. He wasn't an overly large man, and they'd had the foresight to pay handsomely for a little bit of help. If he talked, they would just have to kill the help too. But he wouldn't. He was like them, after all. A utilitarian, and he believed in the higher cause of humanity—the greater good and all the sacrifices it required. A true disciple of Jeremy Bentham.

She was laughing now, that contagious flutter, and it got them really going. They all began to laugh, including the man they had hired, his enormous hulk stuffed into the backseat alongside their victim. They drove down the road into the advancing dusk, her hands outstretched—those nails, the wind whipping through that cinnamon hair.

And for a moment, just the briefest of moments, it was as though you could just reach out and touch her again, *as if she were still alive*. It was enough to break your heart.

6

LILLIE

Nanny White was awaiting their arrival as Harry's car sidled up to Orchard Cottage and deposited its four passengers in front. Lola was awake and making gurgling noises at a contented Primrose who had seen fit to hold her in her arms in the back seat the entire journey from the station. Lillie and Harry got out of the car while Prim looked as though it was the last thing in the world she was willing to do. Eventually she ceded and joined them.

Nanny White was a middle-aged woman with an overly exaggerated hourglass figure, a tight, salt-and-pepper bun, and a kindly round face. Relieved, Lillie stepped forward to greet her.

"Oh, Miss Mead, such a lovely delight to finally meet you. And this is baby Lola? Ah..." She reached out to relieve Primrose of her bundle but Prim deftly avoided handing over the baby. Lillie hid her amusement. "Well, I'll just help you get settled then, shall I?" Nanny White adjusted accordingly, not missing a beat.

Rumple had brought the cases around the side of the car and was now carrying them into the cottage. Nanny followed closely behind. Lillie stared contentedly up at her cottage. The windows had been recently washed and they reflected the setting sun, the garden was blooming, her pathway weeded and swept. She hadn't known that Harry was going to build her an entire guest cottage to help ease her and Lola back into Oxford life and she linked her arm through his now as they walked together to the front door.

"Harry, it's too much! An entire cottage? But, really, thank you," she whispered to him.

"Don't be silly; I can't believe you've gone this long without help."

"I haven't had a baby until now."

"Yes, well, about that. Did you just decide one day after tea that adopting a baby would be a good idea—on your own, no less?"

"Not quite." She wondered how much she wanted to elaborate and decided that for the moment, the less said, the better. "And anyway, I am hardly alone, I have you two."

"Some people just get a puppy, you know." He glanced behind them at Primrose, who was in a complete other world from theirs. Lola had utterly mesmerized her and the two of them gazed at one another as though they had each found their counterpoint. "Although I do rather wonder if Nanny White will be superfluous with Prim around." He raised one sharp eyebrow.

Lillie knew from Primrose's tear-soaked letters over the past half year that Harry and she weren't able to have children of their own. They had seen every London doctor possible and the prognosis was always the same. It just wouldn't be possible. It was tragic, really; so many people were unfit parents and had loads of children and the one couple that really deserved them couldn't have them.

Harry was still chatting on as they entered the main cottage. "Will you be up for dining with us this evening. I've invited

Superintendent Petters as well. Poor chap has missed you terribly. He turned up here today wanting to speak with you about something that's happened in Henley; no idea what, he's as secretive as a young nun sneaking a village boy into the vestibule."

"Of course, thank you, that would be nice. Although I might not bring Lola. I do try to make sure she gets down at a proper hour so she isn't exhausted and miserable in the morning." She oddly felt comfortable with Nanny right away and knew she would take excellent care of Lola just as soon as Primrose saw fit to let her go. "It does seem rather decadent to have another hand; the past few months have been exhausting." She had barely slept since Lola had been born and the intermittent sleep was catching up to her. She fought the urge to yawn and lie down right where they stood.

Lillie went into the kitchen and dropped her bag on the kitchen table. The entire room smelled of flowers and lemon soap. She smiled, turning to hug her two best friends. The three of them stood huddled in the kitchen around the ivory bundle in Primrose's arms. They didn't hear Nanny White arrive in the room behind them.

Carefully and diplomatically, she said, "Mrs Green, would you mind if I held the baby? Just for a moment, so I can get to know her?"

They looked up, startled at the voice, and Primrose nodded. She walked towards her and delicately handed over the bundle in her arms.

"Yes, of course. But just for a moment," she cautioned.

7

"You want to kiss me," the girl teased, drawing her long fingers along the sweater of the most handsome boy at the university. It was nearly dark and she could just make out his outline in the moonlight reflected off the River Cherwell.

He leaned forward, as though he wanted to inhale her, sniffed, then raised his chin as though it would dampen temptation. It was nearly animalistic. He would draw it out. Or try to. She couldn't see his eyes, but she knew from staring into them, day after day, that they would be boring a hole right through her. The thought made her heart leap. He wasn't hers, not even close—but he had feelings for her, this she knew. Strong feelings. She thought of the girl he went around with, smart yes, but unpleasant and spiteful. She visualized her thin eyebrows and broad nose, her nasty downturned mouth and wide forehead and she knew, as he did, that she was the very opposite of her—*in every conceivable way.*

She turned away from him and knew he would follow her. They had that, a cord between them. A secret attachment no one knew about—not her friends, nor his. A backroom arrangement, a clandestine friendship, a furtive glance, a stolen hour. She could hear the grass crunch under their feet. They were near *Tim's Boathouse* and they crept past it, the stars shone yellow above them. She reached behind her and felt for his hand. He pulled her back to him and tucked her back into his chest, breathed down her neck and nearly lit her ablaze. She could feel his lips brush her skin, his bones pushed back against hers and they fit perfectly, like a jigsaw puzzle.

He would have to go soon, it was always that way. But she tried not to let it bother her, even though it invariably did. She wondered, not for the first time, how she would ever get over loving him. It was as though that cord between them was permanent and neither of them had the power to cut it.

She tripped and stumbled forward over something soft that was buried under the grass. He laughed and reached out to catch her. *Clumsy girl.*

"Oh, ugh, it's an animal. A dead animal." She exclaimed, feeling instantly sick. The fur was gone and she could just make out the pinkish-white skin underneath.

"Careful," he righted her, steering her around it then stopping to have a better look. "I don't see fur..." He echoed her thoughts, then knelt down beside it and pushed away the grass. "Acch," he recoiled, suddenly standing up.

"What is it?"

"Don't look. Keep walking. Head back and call the police. Can you go alone? I better wait here."

"But, I don't understand, what is it?"

"It's human. Part of a human."

"No!"

"Go quickly."

The girl turned and picked up a run, feeling her blonde hair fan out behind her as she sprinted back across the meadow towards Lady Margaret Hall.

8

LILLIE

Dinner at Tynesmore had been cut short. Lillie felt her stomach growl in protest as she stood in the dark with a uniformed officer on the edge of the meadow near the River Cherwell. A ring of lanterns had been set up around the remains and she watched as Felix Petters barked orders to his underlings.

"I want a full sweep of the area, the entire meadow and a dredge of the river bed, do you understand. Begin at first light —no point doing it now and missing something. And have the entire circumference"—he gestured a wide arc with his hand —"cleared of onlookers immediately. As far as we know, there aren't any witnesses in that group so unless I'm wrong, I want them gone." Petters motioned to Lillie to join him before remembering something. He turned back to his officers. "Oh, and mind the animals in our area. The last thing I want is a dog running off with a piece of him. Are we clear?" A chorus of *yes sirs* came from his deferential crew.

Petters nodded at them. The young man who had found the remains was sitting a little way away on a blanket alone and Petters made his way over to him.

"Son?" Petters said, while Lillie hurried to join him, thinking she should really get back home and sleep while she could. Lola rose early.

The young man looked up.

"You were the first on the scene?"

The man nodded.

"Were you alone?"

He gave Petters a resistant look which Lillie read instantly and Felix missed entirely. Lillie looked up at the amassing crowd and watched as a stout, dark-haired female student was having harsh words with one of the junior officers manning the perimeter. The young man followed her eyes and nearly winced. The girl was waving her arms towards them and the officer shook his head.

Petters persisted. "Son?"

"No."

"Who were you with?" The notebook was out and Petters flipped the page and started a new one.

The young man looked at the infuriated woman on the perimeter again, then reluctantly answered, "Genevieve Marks."

"And is she here?" Petters followed the young man's gaze. "Is that her?"

"No. She isn't here."

"Where can we find her?"

"Lady Margaret Hall."

"Fine, thank you. Now, you were out here with Miss Marks and you just came across the remains?"

"Yes. Genevieve stumbled over something in the grass, we thought it was a dead animal and then I realized it...wasn't."

"Did you see anyone? Anyone else out here?"

"No, it was just us."

"How long were you in the meadow?"

"Not long, about an hour or so. We had come from campus

and just wanted to—" He broke off, glancing at the woman on the perimeter who had her arms crossed and was glaring towards them now, her face lit up by the police lanterns. "Spend some time," he finished.

Petters nodded, scribbling something in the notebook.

"Where is the rest of...it?" the young man asked, nodding towards the remains.

The severed arm was still lying in the field and the coroner had just arrived. He was hovering over it now, back hunched, glasses perched on his avian-like nose. Lillie recognized him from Petters' other cases. The man removed a handkerchief from his back pocket and wiped at his forehead, then set back to work.

"We don't know, not yet." Petters gave him a dismissive nod. "Constable Richmond will take your details." He motioned to an officer who hurried their way.

Petters winked at Lillie to suggest they were finished with the young man and the two of them walked to the perimeter of the field.

"Twice in a week," he said. "First Henley, now this. Not much of a homecoming for you."

"Was the rest of the body in Henley ever found?"

"Pieces. Some in the river, some in one of the boathouses. We did manage to get an identification on him—I didn't get the chance to tell you all this before we were called out tonight. His name is Edwin Hastock. Or was."

"From Oxford?" Lillie asked.

"Yorkshire, actually, but he's been in Oxford for years. He was a spare rower, not regular squad. Had been at one time but he's a few years older than the lads they have there now." Petters ran his hand across his scalp.

"And still at the university?"

"Yes, pursuing his doctorate. A bit of a regular fixture

there," he confirmed. "Seems to have been the education that went on and on, rather."

"Why would someone want him dead? And then to dismember him like that..." The thought made Lillie shudder.

"No idea at this point. Will you be covering this for the newspaper?"

Lillie gave him a smirk. "Felix, I've only been back in Oxford for a total of about eight hours after six months abroad. I've no idea what Jeremy wants at this point. And to tell you the truth, I've been thinking about giving it all up and writing novels. I could be at home more, with Lola now—"

"Nonsense. You will be bored stiff," Petters countered, interrupting her. "And Jeremy won't be able to survive without having you at the newspaper. I saw him a few times while you were in France; he covered your workload so he wouldn't have to hire someone else. Did you know that?"

"I had heard," Lillie answered. Her boss, Jeremy Winston, had become a loyal friend. She had received a package every week from him while she was in Provence. He would carefully fold each day's issue of the *Oxford Daily Press*, tie them with string then box them. On top of the issues would be a handwritten letter in his impeccable penmanship detailing whatever the goings on at the newspaper had been. He always signed off with the assurance that she would have her post of lead crime reporter when she returned. Of course, he had no idea at that point that she would be returning with a baby in tow.

"He's missed you terribly." Petters winked.

It was generally accepted knowledge in their circle that Jeremy held a torch for her.

"Hush," she admonished. "Now, I must go; it's nearly one a.m. and Lola will be waking soon." She stifled a yawn. "I'll speak with you tomorrow."

"Good, get some sleep."

9

LILLIE

Nanny White's guest cottage had the drapes drawn wide open to the early morning sunshine. Lillie had just woken after a groggy couple of hours of sleep. She had written her article hastily in the dimly lit and nearly empty newspaper office into the wee hours of the morning, dropping it with the overnight typesetter before dragging herself home. She hesitated on the stoop for just a moment before she raised her hand to knock. A waft of fresh scones and wet tea leaves greeted her as the door was flung wide.

"You poor thing, you must be exhausted. Please, no need to ever knock, come in, come in." Nanny White hurried back into her minuscule but perfectly outfitted kitchen, courtesy of Harry Green, motioning for Lillie to follow.

A straw bassinet sat on the kitchen table and Lillie could hear the satisfied coos of baby Lola. She reached in and gathered up her baby girl, showering her with gentle kisses. It had been the first night she had ever spent apart from her.

"Just as good as a lamb," Nanny White was saying as she puttered between the stove and the pantry. "She slept until six this morning. Poor thing must have been exhausted from the travels, aren't you, pet?" she murmured to Lola who gave a satisfied sigh as though she were on cue. The two of them were already becoming fast friends and Lillie felt the relief that any new mother has when they have someone they trust to lighten the load.

Nanny pulled the source of the delicious smell from the oven and placed a hot tray of scones on top of the stove. She set to work spooning jam from a jar Lillie recognized as one of Primrose's and put a few of the scones on a delicate china plate decorated with a rim of irises. Placing them on the table beside Lola's bassinet she urged, "Please, eat something. You are as thin as bird in winter."

"Presumably they go south though, so who would know?" Lillie teased, taking a scone and smothering it in jam.

"Oh! I nearly forgot. You had a visitor last night. Quite late actually, I nearly didn't open the door."

Lillie chewed carefully, feeling the scone catch in her throat. She knew who it was before Nanny White even continued.

Nanny put another scone on Lillie's plate. The woman was trying to fatten her up. "Although he was perfectly charming when I did," she said, apparently oblivious of Lillie's discomfort. "A Mr Wexler. American, by the sound of his accent. Said he worked with you in some capacity and needed the notes for a story you were doing in conjunction with one another?" Nanny White smiled her ignorance and Lillie wondered for a split second if the woman could see right through her. "Terribly handsome man—in a slightly terrifying way." She gave a short-lived chortle. "I don't know why I said that! But working with him must be quite something." The woman winked at Lillie and set to fussing with Lola's blankets.

Lillie didn't need to ask if he had said he would return. Daniel would do as he damn well pleased. She thought of their last night together in Provence, two months previous. He had been leaving for New York and attempting to coerce her to go with him, to which she had flatly refused, telling him instead that she would be returning to Oxford as planned. Whatever was calling him back to America must have been vitally important or she really didn't think he would have left. He never told her what it was, and they had parted in a flurry of frustration and heated kisses. His grey eyes, flat and angry at the time, had terrified her. Her skin tingled just thinking about it.

There hadn't been a word from him since and she had forged on without him, realizing that deep down she would need to imagine a life without him if she was to return to England. A wanted man there, he certainly wouldn't be able to join her. She'd had to make some hard decisions while she sat in that Provencal cottage, staring out of its mullioned windows past the old washboard sink and fading floral curtains. It was either Daniel or her life in Oxford—her friends, the newspaper, her work, her home. It hadn't been an easy decision, nor a satisfying one, but it was one she needed to make and she had chosen her carefully-built life and Lola. The last thing they could be was a cozy little family. He was an ex-assassin, after all, and he could hardly expect that people from his past weren't going to come for him. She shook off the chill that thought gave her.

So, he was back and looking for her. Lillie inhaled deeply and realized Nanny White was studying her. She swallowed the piece of scone that had lodged itself in her throat, reaching for her tea to wash it down.

"I expect he will be back," Lillie said carefully. "In the meantime, I have a few errands this morning." She gathered up a gurgling Lola and planted kisses on her cheeks, rejoicing in the simple pleasure of a baby's scent and pushing Daniel from her mind.

"I can imagine there must be so much to do having just returned. Miss Lola and I will take a walk this morning before it gets too warm," Nanny White assured her, gathering the dirty plates and placing them with a clatter in the sink. "I have things completely under control here, don't you worry about a thing. Oh, I almost forgot, Mrs Green also called this morning and requested some time with Lola this afternoon at Tynesmore." Lillie smiled. "You'll have a battle on your hands with Primrose around. She won't give this baby up." Lillie cradled Lola and placed her gently back in her bassinet. She had made the right decision to come back to Oxford.

THE *OXFORD DAILY PRESS* offices in Cornmarket Street were airless and stale smelling.

"You have got to open some windows!" Lillie scolded, moving around the reception area and pushing open a bank of them behind the waiting area. "And if you prop open the door you can get a cross breeze. Have you got something heavy?"

Her boss, Jeremy Winston, his thin body draped over the reception counter, raised one eyebrow, adjusted his glasses, and smirked at her. "I was starting to think you would never return."

"And no secretary today?" Lillie ignored him.

"I'm having trouble finding a suitable candidate."

Jeremy had the most difficult time keeping staff.

"Because you are demanding, impatient, and intolerable?" she retorted.

"Perhaps. But I am terribly glad you are back. You look... different, somehow."

"Hardly."

"In a good way, I mean you are always good—" He began to get flustered and changed the subject. He placed that morning's paper in front of her on the empty reception desk and pointed to her article. "You are going to need to link the two deaths— obviously it's the same killer," he stated, flatly.

Lillie noticed again that the tip of his right index finger was partially missing. He had told her once of an accident with an axe when he had been younger but she had forgotten it until now. She studied the rounded scarred tip noting the tell-tale criss-cross of faded stitch marks where a nail should have been.

"Not obviously," she answered him. "Two different towns, miles apart. Two different sets of body parts. A severed head and a severed arm. Superintendent Petters would be furious with me if I were to do that and fuel speculation and hysteria. Facts first, Jeremy. We aren't in the business of supposition." She glanced around the office, then glared at him. "Unless this is now *The Mail* and I am a society reporter?"

He persisted. "Have you looked into the background of these two chaps? Both Oxford students, there has to be something more to this."

It was unusual for Jeremy to be so insistent when she had already presented her case to him. Normally, she made an argument and he went along with it. "Am I no longer head crime reporter?" she asked with creeping annoyance. Perhaps she had been away so long he had forgotten how they worked.

"Of course you are. You know I said you could have your job back when you returned."

"So why are you overriding me on this?" she questioned him. "And how do you know both victims were Oxford students? Petters certainly doesn't know this, at least not yet."

Jeremy looked somewhat perplexed. "Well, we know the first was and I just assumed that because the second one was found on university grounds..." He trailed off, seemingly unsure.

Lillie studied him. He seemed anxious somehow, as though something was bothering him. Was it her article or something completely unrelated? "Is everything alright with you?" she asked.

"Yes, of course, why do you ask?" He gave the newspaper a shake and set to folding it, avoiding her eyes.

"You just seem a little out of sorts."

"Don't be silly."

"Well anyway," she continued. "I'm going to head over to the police station this morning and see if I can't get an update. I'll be back later."

"Good," said Jeremy, turning away.

Lillie watched his retreating back for a moment, feeling for all the world as though something wasn't quite right.

10

SUPERINTENDENT FELIX PETTERS

"Expertly dismembered?" Jeremiah asked, looking like a young Sherlock Holmes in the making. He was chewing on the end of a pencil—rather than stoking his pipe—to help his concentration, then he let it drop to the desk.

Felix looked at his adopted son and felt extremely proud of him. He watched as the boy swirled the heavily sugared tea around his cup, as though he needed every last granule to dissolve before he would dare to take the first sip. Felix pondered whether or not his own compulsiveness wasn't rubbing off on him·and made a mental note to extinguish it as much as possible when the boy was around. Jeremiah then refocused his attention on the paperwork before him as though it were a school essay in need of an edit. Felix wondered if he was making a mistake by not sheltering the boy from his police work—although if there was any trauma done, he certainly couldn't see it. He seemed as keen and as analytical as any detective Petters had on the force. Perhaps more so.

"According to the coroner, it would seem so." Petters took a sip of his own tea and glanced up at the clock. It was almost noon and they really didn't know much more now than they had known twelve hours ago.

"So, surgically, then." The boy pointed to a paragraph in the coroner's hurried report. Petters had leaned on the man to give them at least an overview by midday and the exhausted man had just delivered his summary of findings. They would have to wait another day for the full report.

"I suppose so, yes," Felix confirmed.

"You know it was covered in the paper this morning."

"I saw that." Felix smiled. "I like Miss Mead. I'm glad she's back. That Winston fellow doesn't seem to have the same—oh, what is it—*flair*, that she has."

Petters wondered if the boy had a passing fancy for Lillie— after all, how many of his peers read the daily newspaper? Well, he was about the right age now. He wouldn't be the first school age boy to fall for an older woman.

A knock on his office door announced the object of their discussion. Petters couldn't help but notice the boy flush crimson as Lillie strode in.

"I was surprised you managed to get that story printed for this morning," Petters said, motioning to the tea tray and deftly ignoring Jeremiah's discomfort. "A cup?"

"Mm, please. I couldn't sleep and I managed to get it written before Jeremy got the presses running. Nothing like being current, although I certainly hope there aren't any errors in it. There wasn't much time for a thorough proofing."

"I do appreciate it. The more witnesses we can pull in, the better. At this point we don't have anyone who has seen anything."

Petters handed her the tea and took his seat. "Sounds like you are back to work, then?"

She nodded and sipped. "Novels can wait, I suppose." She looked around her. "You know, this might be the first time I have ever not shared your office space with a rescued animal."

"We have a badger at home," Jeremiah put in.

"Of course you do." She smiled at him.

"Broken femur, but we think he's got a good chance of survival." The boy sipped his tea thoughtfully, and carried on, "It's his attitude that is going to be a much longer project."

"Yes, but presumably that's badgers for you," Lillie agreed.

"Not necessarily, most are quite fearful of humans. They get their fierce reputation because of their aggressiveness towards one another. Although this one does tend to be a little full of himself."

"I see." Lillie winked, humouring the boy. "Well, if anyone can effect change, young man, it'll be you."

"Having said that," Petters interrupted. "I don't believe that is why you are here, is it?"

"Not really, but I don't mind getting an education on local wildlife. Did you hear the vicar is petitioning the local council to install owl boxes all along the river? It was in the local section of the paper this morning."

"But he's got it all wrong," Jeremiah exclaimed with frustration. "They need to face leeward and he's got them facing windward. And anyway, he certainly isn't going to find barn owls using them—little owls perhaps, or even long-eareds, but it won't be who he expects."

"Do owls need houses, particularly?" Petters asked, immediately regretting it. They had work to do and this was a diversion he didn't need. He silently cursed Lillie.

"If they don't stop cutting down the trees along the river they do," Jeremiah confirmed.

"Which river?" Oh, why was he even asking!

"Well, the Thames obviously." Lillie answered.

"It could have been the Cherwell."

"Speaking of," Lillie continued, finally giving them a reprieve from wildlife. "Anything new on the Oxford death?"

"Assuming it is a death. As of eleven o'clock this morning, we still only have the one arm. Expertly dismembered, incidentally. We were just discussing this when you came in. It is possible the rest of the chap is still alive somewhere."

"How grotesque to imagine." Lillie glanced towards Jeremiah and gave Petters a stern look, presumably to suggest they shouldn't be speaking in front of the boy.

"Son? You should probably get on home. I don't want that badger left alone too long."

"Yes, sir." Jeremiah got up reluctantly and moved towards the door. "Goodbye, Miss Mead, and welcome home."

When he had left the room, Lillie scolded him. "Honestly, Felix, you have to be careful what you say around him. He'll be sure to have nightmares."

"Spoken like a true parent." He smiled at her. "Incidentally, when do I get to meet the new addition?"

"Come for supper this evening with Jeremiah? Assuming you can leave that badger for a few hours."

"We'd be delighted. Now." He got down to business. "I've been in contact with the York police department about our victim at the regatta. They've notified Edwin Hastock's next of kin."

"How tragic. I can't even imagine how they must feel."

"He has an interesting history. Left Yorkshire years ago to pursue his education at Oxford and was an exceptional rower until he injured his arm in an automobile accident. Apparently he plowed his car into the Ouse and just barely managed to swim himself out. A middle-of-the-night thing and there was speculation that there was a lot of whiskey involved. He had his girl with him but she, unfortunately, didn't make it out in time."

"Oh, how awful. What a terribly sad story."

"Have you got a name?"

"Of the girl? Uh, yes, it's here somewhere." He consulted his notes. "A *Flora Stewart*."

"From Yorkshire, or Oxford?"

"Scotland, actually. Edinburgh area. Although she had gone to York that summer with him to meet his parents."

"I assume then they were either engaged, or nearly so. When was this?"

"July, 1920."

"Three years ago."

"Yes," Petters confirmed.

"To the month," Lillie added.

He hadn't thought of that. "What are you getting at?" he asked.

"Probably nothing." Lillie shifted her chair. "Supposition. Anything else on him?"

"I'm heading to the university now to interview an old roommate of his, care to tag along?"

He hardly needed to ask. It was Lillie, after all, and she could never resist a good story.

11

Y*ou must remember that day on the beach?* She laughed, and the wind whipped her hair around her face, a translucent mask of merriment in a sea of cinnamon. They were in the car again and the top was down, the white of the sun beating down on their scalps as they shaded their eyes. The road kicked up a film of dust behind them as the car sped through the countryside. A fine grit lay itself across the hood, steadily thickening with each mile, turning the car's black paint grey, as though they were driving through a motion picture.

"Of course I do." The ache at the memory was nearly unbearable—salt-water-soaked umbrellas warding off the northern winds and failing miserably while the two of them sprinted along a frothing edge of water feeling it soak their clothes and rescue their spirits. The sand rubbing their toes raw. It felt like it was only yesterday.

She raised one gossamer hand, as though to push her hair back, but instead it faded through. It wouldn't be long before she would be gone again. Only by doing this, by taking these steps, could they keep her here. Or so it seemed. She came back stronger after each one.

And so, with herculean intent and a heavy heart, the driver pushed the sports car into the next corner, feeling it skid through the turn, splaying a wake of thin gravel and regret behind them.

The body in the boot rolled along with them.

12

LILLIE

They sat in a small on-campus tea room awaiting the arrival of Edwin Hastock's roommate. The restaurant was nearly empty, owing to the time of year. Most students were on holiday and those that were in residence were much more interested in being outside at this time of year. They nearly had the place to themselves.

"Jeremy was acting a little odd this morning," Lillie said conversationally while she alternated between perusing the tea menu and watching the door.

"Odd how?" Petters asked, closing his menu and wiping the already perfectly clean table in front of him with his napkin. He focused in on one particular spot where the marble had been etched, and rubbed at it.

Lillie gave him a stern look. "It's a stain, Felix, you are wasting your time."

He reluctantly ceased, regretfully placing the napkin in his lap.

She continued. "Jumpy or something. Nervous, even."

"Maybe he's just excited to have you back. Even with that new baby in tow, he'd marry you in heartbeat."

"Don't be silly. And it isn't that. Anyway, I'm hardly looking to get married." She thought of Jack, her ex-fiancé, noting with surprise that he hadn't really crossed her mind much since she had returned to Oxford. And nor had Harry or Primrose spoken of him. It was as though he had just disappeared from their lives. He hadn't, of course, or certainly not from Harry's, but with his work in London and his new—or should she say old and now current again—girlfriend and their child, he was on an entirely new life path. As was she.

A lean young man entered the restaurant and, on seeing Felix's uniform, made his way over to their table.

"Superintendent Petters? I'm David Spool. Hello." He shook Felix and Lillie's hand, and pulled out the extra chair.

When he was seated Felix introduced Lillie. "Miss Mead works for the *Oxford Daily Press* but we assure you, everything we talk about here this afternoon is off the record. She is simply here as my associate."

"That's fine, thank you," said Spool without enthusiasm.

"Can I get you something?" Felix asked the man, as a waiter approached the table.

"Tea, please, with milk."

Petters nodded. "Three of those please." When the waiter had departed he continued, "I'm terribly sorry about Mr Hastock. Were you two fairly good friends?"

"Roommates more than friends, but I enjoyed his company —most of the time."

This perked Lillie's interest. "Oh, what do you mean by that?"

David placed his hands on the table and linked his fingers together. "He was a pleasant enough fellow, often very humorous and light-hearted. He wasn't much one for studying so I used to have to spend most nights in the libraries because he would have our room full of chaps like him."

"Like him?" She persisted.

"He and his friends, rowers mostly, they didn't take things like education very seriously. And they liked their drink. Usually he would have quite the raucous gatherings. Well, not *usually*. Always. That's the thing about people who enjoy their alcohol a little too much, isn't it? There tends to be a fine line between what constitutes an enjoyable evening and the onslaught of darkness. Not only for them, but for everyone around them."

Petters nodded, giving Lillie a sideways glance. "Can you be more specific?"

"He was the most affable chap when he was sober. And a complete contemptible schmuck when he was drinking: belligerent, arrogant, obtuse, sometimes even violent. He'd had more than one warning from the head of house before he died. I don't know why they didn't evict him." He smiled guiltily at them, as though he had said too much. "Still, it isn't fair to slander the dead, is it. For the most part I really liked him."

"I see." Petters nodded. Their tea was delivered and they remained silent while the waiter placed their cups and saucers in front of them and poured from a large china teapot. "What do you know of his accident up in Yorkshire a couple of years ago? Apparently he drove his car into the river?"

Spool nodded. "He didn't often speak of it, only the once, but I'd heard about it in detail from another student who was also from York and knew him. Terribly tragic, it killed his passenger. No doubt the drinking later on had something to do with forgetting, or trying to. That's usually the way, isn't it?"

"Possibly," Petters answered. "Although I rather think the drinking may have been prevalent before the accident."

"Hm." Spool nodded. "I do know that he would receive an anonymous letter each year on the anniversary of the accident."

"Really?" Petters reached into his pocket and retrieved a small notebook and pen.

"Mm. He was rarely there to receive it, being summer holidays and all, so I would sign for it—it was always sent by courier—and place it on his desk until he got back to the dormitory. The first time he received one he went absolutely insane, flew into a rage. That was the only time he ever spoke of what had happened to him, and even then, it was just pieces of the story, never the whole truth. And I didn't pry, it wasn't really my place to do so."

The waiter reappeared at the table. "Superintendent? There is a call for you from the police station."

"Excuse me," he said to the two of them and made his way from the table.

Lillie eyed the young man before her. "And he had no idea who sent the letters every year?"

"If he did, he didn't disclose it to me."

"Do you know if he still has them?"

"I can look in his desk. His family have yet to come pick up his things—the police wanted another day to sort through them. But when I start to box them up I'll keep my eyes open for the letters."

"That's kind of you to pack things for them. I expect it would be quite difficult for the family to come and do all that, in light of what has happened."

"Can I ask you something?" He looked intently at her.

Lillie inclined her head. "Of course."

"Why decapitate him? I mean, who would do that?"

It was a question she had asked herself time and again since Felix had told her of the murder. "Somebody very sick, I would assume. But at the moment, that's a matter for the police to try to piece together and I don't have any more information. I'm sorry."

Spool nodded gravely.

Felix was making his way back to the table and instead of taking his seat he leaned forward to grab his uniform coat. "I'm sorry, Mr Spool, Miss Mead and I are going to have to cut this short."

Lillie was surprised but got up and gathered her things.

"I'll be in touch if I need anything further," Felix said, shaking the man's hand.

As they made their way from the restaurant, Lillie hurrying to keep pace with Petters' determined stride, she asked. "What's happened?"

"We've discovered an armless body on the outskirts of town. Looks like it's been tossed out of a car and left for us to find."

They emerged into sunshine and hastened towards the dark police car Felix had parked at the curb.

THREE HOURS later Lillie found herself back at home in her garden watching the leaves on her hornbeam hedging rustle with an approaching wind. She glanced up at the July sky and noted the ominous creep of dark clouds. They were to have a storm that evening, she thought, as she pushed Lola's pram back and forth in short sweeping movements along the grass. She had hoped for another nap but the baby's delight at watching the goings-on overhead probably meant it was wishful thinking on Lillie's part. She peered closely at the tiny bundle before her and adjusted her blankets for the hundredth time that day.

Nanny White had taken the afternoon to get some household supplies from town and take a bit of a break. Lillie pushed the images of a few hours ago from her mind. A naked, one-armed body, caked in roadside dirt which stuck horrifically to the river of blood that had pooled down one side of his torso and thigh. Dead, obviously, but according to the coroner who was already on scene when they arrived, only fairly recently. He had survived the amputation of his arm, unfortunately, and gone on to live an excruciating existence until he had slowly and painfully bled out.

"Do you think we are dealing with someone who has some medical training?" Lillie asked Felix Petters as he emerged from her kitchen into the garden, balancing a tray of tea and some freshly baked biscuits courtesy of Nanny White.

He deposited the tray on the silver-weathered teak table and began to pour.

"Jeremiah said the same thing to me earlier. It's possible, yes," he agreed. "And looking more and more likely. Edwin's decapitation was too clean for it to have been a complete amateur."

"Although, they did manage to kill our second victim by allowing massive blood loss, so that might disprove that theory," Lillie added, taking a sip of her tea.

"Unless they wanted him to die that way. Let's face it, whoever it is doesn't seem to be in the business of mercy." Petters sighed, and took a seat.

"When do you suppose you might get an identification on the body?"

"We are perusing all missing persons reports for the area now. I assume that someone would have reported a young man like that had he disappeared without a trace."

"I suggest beginning at Oxford University. It's looking increasingly likely that this man and poor Edwin from the regatta are related cases."

Petters reached across the table and took a biscuit from the tray. "It would be odd to have two cases with missing body parts and find them not related, I suppose."

Felix seemed to think about this while he watched Lillie push Lola's pram. He changed the subject suddenly and Lillie had to hurry to catch up. "What made you go and do that after all those months in Provence?"

"Lola?"

He nodded, chewing, wiping crumbs from his fingers.

"We needed each other." Lillie didn't want to give any more specifics than that. She reached for the milk and splashed some in her tea, getting half of it on the table while she did so. "Could you watch her for a moment? She's nearly ready to nod off anyway. I want to get some napkins."

Felix nodded and took over the pram rocking. "We call them 'serviettes' here," he said absently.

"Harry doesn't," Lillie replied over her shoulder as she sprinted across the lawn and into the kitchen. Making her way to the pantry she retrieved a couple of linen cloths from the cupboard. For a moment she stood at the kitchen sink gazing into the yard. She watched as Felix pushed the pram gently this way and that, checking on her baby girl with all the carefulness of a surgeon. A tap on the front door interrupted her thoughts and she went to answer it. She had expected her milk delivery earlier in the day but Nanny White had reported with some frustration that the neighbourhood schedule was all over the map.

Pulling the door open to the heavy heat of an impending afternoon storm, she caught her breath.

"Hello." Daniel stood on the doorstep, one arm on the frame of the door, leaning slightly forward as though it were the most natural thing in the world to show up at her cottage after their time in Provence had come to an abrupt and gut-wrenching end.

She inhaled sharply, looking up into his moody grey eyes and realizing she couldn't decide if she wanted to slap or embrace him. She did neither, struggling instead to compose herself while glancing behind her to make sure Felix hadn't come inside after her.

"You can't be here, Daniel. Superintendent Petters is in the garden with Lola."

"I'll wait then, shall I?"

Surely he was being ridiculous?

"Of course not!"

He gave her a half smile. "You could smuggle me into your bedroom, it wouldn't be the first time."

"I've never 'smuggled' you into my bedroom, you have come quite of your own accord." It wasn't the worst idea, though, she had to admit.

"I've never met her," he said, referring to Lola. "And I'd like to."

"I know," she replied quietly.

"How about it, then?" A raised eyebrow over a chiseled face that looked sharper and more gaunt than the last time she had seen it. On second reflection, she thought, he looked exhausted —shadows circled his eyes and she felt herself momentarily weaken.

She sighed, standing back to allow him in. "Quickly."

He brushed past her, letting one hand linger on her arm as he did so. He silently took the stairs two at a time and disappeared from her view.

The telephone began to ring from the kitchen and she rushed to answer it.

"Hello?"

"Miss Mead, it's the Oxford Constabulary, is Superintendent Petters with you?"

"He is, just a moment and I'll get him."

She hurried back into the garden, still holding the napkins. "Telephone call for you from the station."

Petters nodded and released the pram to Lillie. She glanced up at the first floor windows as he made his way to the kitchen. There wasn't any sign of movement, and she exhaled her relief. Lola had drifted off to sleep, her cherub face turned to one side, tiny lips puckered. She had the most delicate eyelashes, and Lillie studied them for the thousandth time. Overhead, the sky darkened and in the distance, over the fields, she could see a swath of gauzy grey hit the neighbouring farms. She turned the pram and headed towards the house. It would be raining within minutes.

Reaching the kitchen she pushed the entire pram inside so as not to wake Lola and loitered outside the telephone alcove while Felix finished his call. He came out and stood before her.

"I think we may have an identification on our body."

"Oh? That's quick."

"Andrew Baker. Oxford student, as you surmised, or was. He had just graduated. He was reported missing by his roommate when he failed to return to pack his things. He had been working in a restaurant in town, closing up on the evening shift, and he never returned. The description matches."

"Pack his things? Where was he going?"

"This is where it gets interesting. Back to York."

"Really? Two deaths of young men from the same town? Do you think he and Edwin Hastock knew each other?"

"It's possible. Look, I better get back. Thank you for the tea."

"My pleasure." She thought of Daniel upstairs and was relieved Felix was leaving.

"Oh, and I don't have to tell you, I don't want any of this in the papers until I can get some firmer answers."

"Of course not."

When he had left, Lillie pushed the pram to the base of the stairs and carefully lifted a sleeping Lola. She gingerly crept up the stairs with her. When she entered her room Daniel was sitting on the end of the bed. He immediately stood, towering over the two of them. Lillie looked up into his granite face and saw something in it that she had never seen before as he gently took the baby from her arms and cradled her to his chest—it was tenderness. He pulled Lillie towards him and gently wrapped his other arm around her, kissing her hair. They stood there for what seemed like forever, the three of them, in that bedroom, gauzy curtains blowing in the summer storm that had begun to rage outside the windows and for a moment Lillie felt that everything was right in the world.

13

I t happened like this sometimes.

The fading smile, the instantly mistrustful eyes, the loss of her innocent gaiety. She would grip the dashboard, the white flecks in her nails erased by the blanching of her fingertips. Her cinnamon hair would fall flat against her cheeks and her chest would heave, as though for all her worth she could no longer breathe away the pain of the world. It was then that it would come: that low, tormented wail from the depths of her soul, starting as a slow roll, then gaining momentum, until it broke loose and shook her entire body, unleashing a broken fury so magnificently frightening that the leather of the car's seats seemed to vibrate beneath her, as they did now.

When it was finished they would sit there, side by side, until she could smile again. And she would, eventually, for that was who she ultimately was. An optimistic soul who saw the good in the world, what little of it there was. It had been a momentary lapse, a mistake—if only they could go back and change it all. If only there had been the faith that it would all pass and eventually fade. If only she had *believed* that she could live through it.

Cornmarket Street was alive with the rain, it hailed down in a sheet, bouncing off the pavement and rushing to puddle—finding any hollow and filling it with its watery sweetness, a mixture of recently cut grass and liquified sunshine. The mosquitos would be sure to arrive shortly after it had finished, they reflected in unison, then smiled.

It was hot in the car and the humidity made their legs stick to the seats. The door of the building they watched across the street opened from time to time, a steady flow of ins and outs, reporters no doubt, and suppliers. Oxford's esteemed storytellers and plebeian ink pedlars.

She was calmer now, the light fading, and they sucked on sweeties to take their minds off the past. Bitter lemon and tart cherry cut their tongues and sweetened their breath. It was reconnaissance only today. It had been a busy week, after all, and they needed some time to formulate an iron-clad plan. She was fading now and in the dark of the storm she glowed nearly white against the dark leather of the car seat. The white slowly morphed into a silvery grey and then an opaque gunmetal, until eventually all that remained was the ashen-coloured leather of the car seat where her legs had once been, and the tangled mess of memories she left in her wake.

The door of the *Oxford Daily Press* opened once again and this time their target teetered on its threshold—he often worked late into the evening, they reflected. A flick of the wrist showed a watch's ebony hands reading seven thirty.

14

LILLIE

Early the next afternoon Lillie, Harry and Superintendent Felix Petters sat in the blissfully cool dining room at Tynesmore mulling things over. It was already too warm to be on the stone patio overlooking the horse fields and Harry had promptly asked Rumple to move the entire lunch back indoors. A cross breeze now blew through the ground floor of the handsome house, each and every window having been thrown open to capture the recently cleaned air. The previous evening's storm had turned everything just a little fresher and brighter. A nearly fluorescent green grasshopper landed on the freshly pressed tablecloth and Harry raised one eyebrow at his manservant. They all watched in silence as it once again took flight and catapulted itself onto the stacked lemon-yellow curtains, disappearing into one of the folds.

Lillie frowned. "Whoever did it must have been very strong. They would have had to drag that body out of the field after they cut off the chap's arm. And unless he was unconscious, he must have been screaming up a storm."

She was putting the final touches to her story, or rather

Felix's story, as she had come to think of it since he seemed to be dictating what she could and could not report. She rolled her pencil across the dining-room table in thought.

They had only just finished luncheon and the plates had been cleared and the dessert laid.

"There is no evidence that he was dragged out of that field. We would have seen blood elsewhere and we didn't. Nor was there any sign of pulling anything along the grass. It was extremely long, we would have seen it," Petters answered.

Harry flicked his hair back and tucked into his second helping of plum tart. It was astounding he didn't ever seem to put on any weight. He looked just as light and athletic as he always had. "I don't suppose he would have walked out. Would be terribly inconvenient after just having one's arm severed. Although I suppose we had a great many boys who did just that during the war." Here he paused, fork poised, as though he were thinking of stabbing an enemy soldier with it. "Or presumably they were carried out by the medics." He concluded with a flick of the fork, taking another bite.

Petters continued, "No, whoever is doing our killing took Andrew Baker from the restaurant that night, amputated his arm, and purposely disposed of it in that field near the river. I don't believe the rest of him was ever there."

"Which would mean two things: the killer has somewhere where he is doing the killing. And he wanted that body associated with the university, for some reason."

"Mm," Petters agreed. "Although, in the case of the regatta, Edwin was surely killed aboard the boat we found his head in and then the rest of his body disposed of in the river."

"Shell," Harry interjected.

Petters looked confused.

"It's referred to as a shell, not a boat," Harry clarified. "Incidentally, has Primrose absconded with that little bundle of love of yours? I haven't seen her since the salad. No doubt she has her tucked into that upstairs nursery she's just finished decorating. I daresay the apple-green walls might have been a bit of a cock-up, I personally voted for the rose pink but there you have it. Always overruled by a woman." Harry got up to pour himself another whiskey from the sideboard. He motioned to Petters, who declined with a slight shake of his head, and a glance at his watch.

"I thought it quite pretty," Jeremiah piped up and Lillie realized she had almost forgotten the boy was there. He had been so quiet enjoying each and every course the footman brought that he had nearly faded into the wallpaper.

Lillie moved on from the boat discussion. "Have we any confirmation that the two victims knew one another?"

"Not yet; working on that," Petters confirmed. "I'll go back and speak again to David Spool, Edwin's roommate, and see if he can't shine any light on it for us. Oh, and incidentally Harry, you mentioned you knew the coxswain?"

"Mm." Harry swallowed. "Will Andrews."

"I'll need to speak with him too."

"Good," Lillie agreed, straining to see the grandfather clock in the hallway outside Harry's dining room. "In the meantime I'll have to put in an appearance at the newspaper this afternoon if I want what little I have of a story to be published in tomorrow's papers."

"Leave Lola here, if you like. Primrose would like nothing better than to dote on her for the afternoon," Harry put in, reaching for another slice of tart.

BY THE TIME Lillie reached the offices of the *Oxford Daily Press* it was nearly two o'clock. She made her way directly to Jeremy's office to find him not there. Backtracking past tables of typewriters and bowed heads, she stopped at the reception desk and asked a woman she hadn't ever seen, but was presumably today's secretary, if she knew his whereabouts.

"He hasn't been in yet today, miss."

"Really? It's the middle of the afternoon." That was so unlike Jeremy it instantly caused the hair on her arms to stand up.

"And terribly inconvenient too," the woman replied. "I was supposed to be trained on the front desk and now I've no idea how to work the telephones or anything else here!"

"Is he sick?"

"I don't know, miss. He hasn't called and I had one of the all-night reporters call him first thing when I arrived and we didn't get an answer. I've just tried him again and same thing, no answer. Oh, I almost forgot, a courier brought an envelope for you. I've put it on your desk."

Lillie nodded a distracted confirmation and headed back through the newsroom to her desk. The reporter beside her nodded a brief hello and then put his head back down, the steady clack-clack of the keys beneath his fingers announcing the imminent arrival of his deadline.

She pulled out her chair and sat heavily into it while she pulled a large envelope towards her. Her name was scrawled across the front of it in a leaden hand but there was nothing to suggest who had sent it. Slicing the top open with her letter opener she peered inside. There was something bulky which was wrapped in gauze and she carefully pulled it out, placing it on the desk before her. The reporter beside her raised his head again with a perplexed look and she fought back an irrational apprehension. She reached back into the envelope looking for a note but found it empty. She raised her eyebrows at the reporter beside her and in the silence under his gaze, she began to unravel the gauze.

The item dropped to the desk suddenly and it took both of them a minute to decipher what they were looking at. Lillie realized it before her co-worker did, but only because she had studied it a few days ago. It was a severed right index finger. She could understand how the reporter next to her didn't realize it right away. Where the nail should have been was the years-old scar where it had been lobbed off and hastily restitched—the criss-cross scars were white against the rest of the tissue, which had begun to turn a putrid shade of purple.

"Oh!" The reporter leapt off his seat and backed away. "Is it? Oh, oh…"

A small crowd had morphed around Lillie's workspace and they crowded in to see what had caused such a commotion.

Lillie stood up abruptly, leaving the finger on the desk. "Don't touch it!" she said to everyone and no one in particular. The nearest phone was in Jeremy's office and she rushed towards it, fighting down the sick feeling in her stomach. Snatching up the receiver she hastily dialled.

"Oxford Police Station," came an efficient voice over the line.

"Superintendent Felix Petters, please," Lillie asked hurriedly.

"He isn't in at the moment, can I give him a message."

"Yes, it's Lillie Mead, I need him to meet me at the following address…it's urgent."

15

Т he screams were getting on their nerves. Admittedly, it hadn't been the plan they had agreed on but sometimes opportunities present themselves and one must adapt.

She was covering her ears, that fine hair of hers falling flatly around her hands and obscuring the white flecks of her nails. There was quite a lot of blood, which wasn't surprising, all things considered. A shot of morphine might silence things, but did he deserve it? Not really. They would just have to wait until he lost consciousness, if he ever did. Well, he couldn't very well scream forever and even if he did, they were so remote no one would hear him.

Shall we leave him here and take a drive?

She nodded her filmy head, the white was robust today, but she wasn't happy.

It's necessary, my love. And the pain will pass.

Hers or his?

Her hazel eyes were fixated on the reporter and she didn't seem to be listening. He couldn't see her, that was obvious enough in the way he looked wildly around him, searching for a way out, no doubt. He'd have to get out of those chains first and that wasn't very likely now, was it?

He deserves this, we always knew he needed to be part of it. He's as much to blame for what happened—after all, it was his choice to not print it. We begged him, pleaded even. How dare he!

There was a familiar anger that began to rise like bile but it was hardly the time for losing one's temper.

They looked down at the thin man in the brown suit, now dirty from his writhing on the floor of the abandoned building, his glasses smashed and lying a few feet to his left. His bigger concern should be the infection that would inevitably come if that wound wasn't kept clean. It could be stitched now, but they didn't feel like doing it. He could bleed a little more.

Let's go, it's a beautiful afternoon, with the sweetest hint of a breeze. I want to take another drive around town, possibly have a picnic on the river's edge? We could stop at that little delicatessen we love, the one with the red-and-white striped awning, and pick up some sandwiches and a bottle of French Burgundy. Let's go. Leave him, my love, just leave him.

She stretched out one delicate, ghostly arm in agreement. The open road awaited them.

16

SUPERINTENDENT FELIX PETTERS

"Lillie?" Silence ensued, so he tried again, a little louder this time. "Lillie! Are you here?"

Jeremy Winston's house was located on a small road to the west of the village. It was a cottage, really, more than a house, and it befitted a man who spent most of his time at the office. It had one bedroom, a small lavatory and a kitchen that appeared to have been abandoned long ago. What little furniture he had placed in the diminutive drawing room he had arranged with the bare minimum of thought. It didn't look as though the room had ever actually been sat in, much less dusted. Thick cobwebs criss-crossed the hallway between it and the kitchen.

"He never used it," said a voice behind him. Lillie, reading his thoughts, came around the darkened corner into the light of the kitchen where Petters was standing. "I've never known him to eat at home. Honestly, if I hadn't already checked there, I would absolutely expect to see him sitting in Beatrice McClaire's bistro across Cornmarket Street right this minute. His office window practically looks directly into the dining room. She can tell by his salivating what he wants for lunch and dinner before he does." She glanced around them at the dismal space, then choked back a cry. "He should have married the woman." She wiped at her eyes and Felix moved forward to console her.

"You don't know he won't still," Petters said gently. "Although I rather think the poor woman will have to compete for space in his heart and mind with you, my dear."

"No..." She wiped away a few huge tears that had rolled down her cheeks with a furious swipe across her face. "Felix, I am so angry. Who is doing this? We have nothing, no leads..."

He nodded. "We are getting there, Lillie. Obviously this makes it that much more urgent. But it also tells me whoever is behind this is motivated by something that was either public in the newspaper or they wanted it to be."

"I can't understand why anyone would take him? I mean the other two, assuming they are related cases—which I believe they are since amputation seems to be the favoured course of action—were Oxford University students."

"It's got to be a story he is either working on or has worked on in the past. The dilemma being, if it is in the past, how far back does it go?" He scratched at his chin.

"Yes, but in the meantime we need to search every single building in Oxford! He could be out there bleeding and suffering, assuming he's even alive."

"It isn't a good use of resources, but of course, we will begin a door-to-door search," he agreed, mentally doing a quick review of staffing for the day. He would need community volunteers if they were going to be effective in any real way.

"And I will go back to the newspaper and root around his office. Maybe there is something there—he was acting strangely the other day, perhaps something has happened recently."

"Good. Do that. In the meantime, I am going to attempt to get in touch with Flora Stewart's family."

"The girl who was in the car that went into the river in York?"

"Yes."

"How is that relevant now, Felix? Edwin Hastock's accident was years ago—do you really think someone lopped off his head because of it? Seems a bit far-fetched."

"It's a start, Lillie. We are looking for a start. Let's talk later this afternoon after you've had a chance to sift through Jeremy's office."

ARRIVING BACK at the police station, Felix marched through the reception, noting his favourite secretary was on duty. She gave him a nod as she lifted a coffee cup with one enormous forearm. The woman was built like a freight train and had a personality to match. It was what made her the perfect hire for the front desk at a police station. Not long after he had hired her, she had single-handedly wrestled a drunkard they had brought in on disturbing-the-peace charges. The man had managed to evade his handcuffs while she was doing his processing and had made a run for the door. The arresting officer had been slow off the mark and the secretary had quickly come around the side of the glassed reception desk and quite calmly tackled him, holding him down with one colossal knee while the arresting officer composed himself and managed to get the handcuffs back on. This time properly.

Having her on duty that afternoon would certainly make organizing a search party of volunteers to find Jeremy Winston a little easier. When he had finished giving her the bare minimum of instruction, noting that she rarely, if ever, needed things spelled out for her, he made his way down the polished hallway floor to his office and shut the door.

Two dead. One missing. All with severed body parts of some sort. He would have the medical examiner have a look at

Jeremy's finger just to make sure they were dealing with the same person, but he hadn't any doubt that they were. He pulled the finger from his pocket and placed it in a small metal ice box behind him.

Then he reached across the desk and picked up the phone to call the Stewart family in Edinburgh.

"Primrose will look after her. She would like nothing better than to step in while we head to Bath." Harry leaned back on the sofa in Lillie's cottage that evening and stretched his long arms behind his head. "We'll stay at the Empire Hotel, I should think. A bit of a monstrosity, but the location is fairly good. I can feed the swans while you meet with the good doctor. Or perhaps not so good." He seemed to consider this then changed his mind. "Never mind, I better come with you, the swans can wait. I'll have Rumple book us a suite of rooms."

Lillie had just put Lola to sleep and she puttered around the living room gathering up the day's mess: a couple of baby blankets, a knitted cap, a half-empty teacup, while she reflected on what had come out of Petters' conversation with Flora Stewart's father. The dead girl's brother had become a surgeon, leaving Edinburgh to pursue his career at the Bath Ministry of Pensions Hospital. She picked up Harry's empty whiskey glass and gave the ice cubes a shake. Had he really drank it so fast that the ice hadn't yet had a chance to melt?

"Us?" she asked.

"I'll have another," he said, as though she had actually asked. "And yes, of course. I always accompany you on these sorts of trips."

"It isn't really necessary." She wondered if Harry perhaps needed an occupation of his own. He seemed increasingly bored with the life of a wealthy young aristocrat. And the empty whiskey glasses were becoming increasingly disconcerting. She wondered how Primrose was feeling about Harry's drinking?

A knock on the door interrupted their thoughts. Had Lillie not known Felix was coming, she would have been worried that Daniel might have once again arrived not realizing that she had company. She pulled open the door to the heady evening air and ushered him in. A choir of crickets and a lone baritone bullfrog continued to sound outside the open windows while a sail of warm summer air fluttered at the drapes.

When they were all seated in front of one another, Lillie anxiously asked. "Any news?" She attempted to wipe the expectant look off her face as she knew it would torment the poor man. He was doing his best, after all.

"Not yet. We've got a total of twenty search parties going now and we will have nearly that many again overnight. It's a big town, Lillie, it is going to take time."

"Assuming they still have him in Oxford."

"Yes, there are blocks on all major roads in and out of town, but it is possible we've missed them if they decided to flee."

Lillie handed him a copy of the story she had unearthed on Flora Stewart's death in York.

"The *York Tribune*," Petters stated, flatly. "Was anything run by Jeremy in the *Oxford Daily Press*?"

"No. But that isn't all that unusual. We wouldn't normally cover something that was a local story in a town far from here. I can't believe this has anything to do with Flora Stewart's death. It doesn't explain our second death either. We don't know that Andrew Baker had his arm severed and was left to die on a roadside because he somehow knew the poor, recently decapitated Edwin Hastock." She frowned. "Surely one has to do with the other, I just don't think this is the link—some doctor in Bath."

"Still, I'd rather rule it out. I'd actually not even bother if he wasn't a medical doctor."

"It does rather pique one's interest," Harry piped up. "Who else would be so comfortable with amputation? Or be so proficient at it." He shuddered and drained half the drink Lillie had re poured him.

"There could be anger at Jeremy for not publishing a story about Flora's death," Petters suggested.

"Felix, there could be anger at Jeremy for not publishing any story anywhere!" Lillie sputtered, frustrated. "It isn't logical."

"Murder often isn't," Petters concluded.

"True," she conceded. "I'll leave on the first train for Bath and hope to only be gone the one day. Please," she begged. "Find Jeremy."

WHEN EVERYONE HAD FINALLY LEFT Orchard Cottage it was nearly midnight. Lillie fought the sinking feeling that Jeremy might be dead, or at the very least, in an extraordinary amount of pain. She crept up the stairs to Lola's bedroom and checked that she was still breathing—something she did at least ten times throughout the night. Watching her baby sleep, the moon slicing through a crack in the curtains, she practiced a steady breathing—in and out, in and out—and wondered about the state of the world for her little girl. She thought of Daniel. He had said he would stay nearby, in case she needed him. She didn't *need* anyone, she thought miserably, but she wanted him and it vexed her to think that she couldn't have him in her life. At least not in the life she had now. There was a familiar ache that haunted her. Would she ever get over the man?

Closing Lola's door she crept down the hallway to bed.

LILLIE

Bath had the air of a town preparing for a summer fair. Its golden-fronted buildings nearly glowed under the temperate sunshine while a gentle breeze blew across a still lush Royal Victoria Park, up the crescent and into The Circus, cooling its inhabitants and visitors alike.

Lillie and Harry arrived at the hospital just after lunch and found themselves staring into the serene face of Flora Stewart's older brother. He had the anaemic complexion of one who spent too much time indoors. A colossal man with a thick Scottish accent, he looked as though he would be more at home chopping down immense forests than in the operating theatre —which was where he had evidently been before they arrived. A white mask still hung around his neck and he wore a small cotton cap, which covered most of his fiery red hair.

They had been shown into a small office near the main entrance and given a cup of tepid tea. Harry glanced over at Lillie and gave her a look of utter dissatisfaction as he put it down after the first sip, while Dr Stewart took his seat across from them.

"You want to know about Flora?" He seemed confused as to why they were there. He pushed the cap back from his forehead and tossed it down on the table before him, running his fingers through his hair.

"Yes, that, but also more specifically about her friend, Edwin Hastock."

The doctor grunted his disapproval. "He killed her," he stated flatly. "What else is there to know?"

The flash of anger and grief in his eyes was unmistakable.

"You've heard Edwin has been murdered."

"Yes. My mother wrote to me." He stared directly at them. "It's hardly a loss to the world," he added.

"Did you know him well?" Lillie tried.

"A little. I never liked him." The doctor sighed, leaning back in his chair. "Flora brought him home to Edinburgh just the once."

"What didn't you like about him?" Lillie queried.

Steward sighed again, heavily. "He was your typical Oxford 'good old boy', I suppose. Entitled, took nothing all that seriously. In Edwin's mind, the world existed for his own pleasure and for no other reason. He was really quite simplistic. But I supposed that's how he was raised."

"I see."

"Flora thought he was something special, but she was too young to really know any different."

"And she and Edwin were to be married?"

The doctor gave a cynical laugh. "Oh no, no I doubt it. Edwin's family were sure to expect him to marry someone who ran in their circles. A girl from Scotland from a working-class family wouldn't have been in the cards for him. She was very pretty, our Flora, and smart and funny—but she was a passing fancy for him." He rubbed at his forehead. "I should have never let her run around with him. I blame myself."

Lillie wondered how this man had managed to escape his station and become a surgeon.

As though he could read her mind he answered. "Scholarship. I left on a scholarship. I wouldn't be here otherwise."

"I see." Lillie nodded. She started her next inquiry delicately. It had only been three years since the girl had died and no doubt losing one's sister would still be as raw years later as it was at the time. "And she went to York that summer to meet his family?"

"That was what Edwin would have told her, yes. He was stringing her along, though. It was summer vacation and he wanted someone to get wildly drunk with, I'm sure. He thought she was easy..." He frowned at the memory. "When it came to him, she probably was." He looked up. "As I said, she was young."

"Of course." Lillie didn't really think the doctor before them was a murderer but she had come this far so she needed to continue her line of questioning. "Did you know Andrew Baker?"

"Who?"

"Andrew Baker. He was another Oxford University student, also from York, oddly, who was recently found murdered."

"No. I didn't. Why are you asking me about him?"

"We are trying to ascertain if he and Edwin might have known each other. There are some similarities in the way they were—killed."

"Was he also decapitated?"

"A severed arm," Lillie confirmed.

"Ah," Stewart said, as though he understood. "*That* is why you are here. Two bodies, both with severed pieces. You think I might have been involved in their murders. Who else would be comfortable with surgical amputation, is that right?"

Lillie would have liked to rule him out but there was something about the man that kept her on edge. Perhaps it was the way he refused to apologize for how he felt about Edwin, as though their victim had deserved what had happened to him. Or perhaps it was his unwavering eye contact. Was he challenging her to prove that he had done it? She wasn't entirely sure. She risked a glance at Harry and noticed her friend was studying the doctor too.

She didn't really want to get the doctor's defences up but she forged ahead anyway, prodding. "It's a theory."

"Of course, and a good one. Although if I am a suspect I am flummoxed as to why a police officer would not be sitting here before me now. Instead they send a reporter and her—"

"Associate," Harry put in.

Stewart raised his eyebrows in doubt. "Listen, Miss Mead, I'm a doctor not a killer. I save lives, not end them. You're on the wrong pathway, I can assure you." He stood up, effectively ending their conversation. "I'm sorry you've come all this way for nothing."

Lillie did the same, and held out her hand. Stewart took it and gave it a firm shake. He looked directly at her. "He killed my baby sister, Miss Mead. I don't really give a damn one way or another what happened to Edwin Hastock. As far as I'm concerned he got what he deserved."

With that the doctor left the room.

Harry stood up, stretching. "Well," he said, arms raised. "Not much to go on there. Now what?"

Lillie gave this some thought as she gathered up her bag. "You know the coxswain."

"Of the Oxford team? Yes, as I said to Petters. Will Andrews," Harry confirmed.

"Good. Now we head home and track him down."

"Shouldn't be too hard, he spends an inordinate amount of time in the campus pub. It's no wonder he's never finished his education. Have you ever managed to read Goethe while intoxicated?"

Lillie looked at him, bewildered.

"Well I have, and it's nearly impossible—no matter how much you appreciate *Wilhelm Meister's Apprenticeship.*" He scratched at his chin. "Which in my case is not a whit, but never mind. Shall we eat?"

19

"He won't die. I promise you."

There was a gauzy nod that she understood, but with it came the accompanying look that said she disagreed with the methods. And to be honest, how did they know he wouldn't? They might kill him still, accidentally.

The afternoon was sticky, a heavy air surrounded them while they sat at the shore of the river on an old cotton blanket that scratched at their skin and itched under their palms—they gazed up at a row of empty owl boxes. It was their second picnic in as many days. She hadn't touched her wine and the cheeses had begun to attract insects. They watched as they buzzed and climbed their ebony bodies all over their lunch. Neither of them felt like eating a thing. She waved a translucent hand as though it would help but it did little other than send of waft of hot air swirling around them.

"I do wonder if we should have moved him earlier, though." It was more a thought and less something that should have been said out loud. Doubt never did anyone any good. They had come this far and had so much further to go still. A quick count on their fingers—three down, how many more to go? How many more were there?

A red kite circled above their heads and they watched as it in turn surveyed them—a flutter of milky feathers dipped in ink searching for its prey. And weren't they doing the same? Watching, searching for prey. The bird dipped once, as though in acknowledgement, nearly skimming the water, and then ascended once again as it disappeared over a curve in the river. A breeze had picked up and it rustled the longer grass near the shoreline, releasing fluffs of dandelion seeds and sending them sailing on the warm air.

"But what will we do with him?" she asked, watching as the tufts dispersed, then gazing up at the sun. She didn't even need to shade her eyes and it illuminated her, bouncing off her translucent skin as though it were buffed metal.

The reporter had been a minor complication, this much was true. He hadn't been involved that night, all those years ago. As such, Winston wasn't someone they could treat as they had the others—they were hardly barbarians. They'd had a grievance with him. And this had been their payback—a severed finger for a story unwritten. It was fitting really, albeit in a slightly grotesque way, and they applauded themselves for thinking of it. Although keeping him alive and contained was another matter altogether. Planning wasn't ever their strong suit, and now they had an injured man who seemed to be waning by the day—if he was even still alive. They hadn't checked on him in the past twenty-four hours and nor had they fed or watered him.

"We could let him go now," she argued, tearing her eyes from the river. "He hasn't seen you, you've made sure of that, and he can't see me. He's hardly a threat."

She was a logical girl—she always had been—and injustice wasn't something she was easily persuaded to accept. It was a consideration. Together they mentally calculated how much of them and their hiding places Winston had seen. The car was a complication—but it wasn't insurmountable. It had been stolen anyway, so they could quite easily abandon it and find another. The barn where they had originally kept him had no ties to them, nor did the remote hunting shed where he was now. They could load him up at dusk and roll him out in front of the newspaper office, problem solved. It would free up their time to find the next one, they considered. And they hadn't said anything of value in front of him, had they?

"Yes, my darling, let's do that. But tomorrow—there's so much we must do in the meantime to prepare for it." It was a concession and one that might make her happier.

She smiled into the sun, and it glowed over her face.

Yes, *if* Jeremy Winston was still alive, they would release him.

20

SUPERINTENDENT FELIX PETTERS

He stood on the threshold of the abandoned barn, the sunlight sluicing through the cracks in the walls and the pinholes in the roof. A theatre director would have envied the pattern of light and an artist would have certainly tried to replicate it. The dirt floor still held the smell of animals long gone; the bristle of horse hair, parched cow dung, chicken feathers. Petters screwed up his nose against the dry air.

The middle of the building housed a large open space, while stalls still bedded in ancient oat straw lined one eastern wall. A panicked scurry of something underneath told him the only living thing here now was a nest of mice. A couple of Felix's officers were cruising the perimeter of the building and he could hear their muted murmurs through the derelict walls.

He stepped into the building. They had only just received a tip from a couple of teens who had been using the space as place to stash their stolen liquor and girlfriends. He admired the boys' nerve in coming to him and reporting the swath of blood they had arrived to find in the centre of the open space. He knelt to have a better look. There was a significant amount of it, he noted, pulling on a pair of gloves. The dirt around it had been disturbed as though someone had spent a time thrashing around in it. Could it be an animal? Possibly. He reached into his pocket and retrieved a small jar he had brought from the station for the purpose of sampling. He scooped a small amount into it, careful to take as little dirt as possible. A glint of something caught the light through the roof and he peered closer into the door to have a better look. A piece of broken glass flashed back at him. Putting the sample jar back into his pocket he set to work brushing the dirt from around the broken glass. There was more of it scattered around where he found the first piece, and he attempted to unearth as much of it as he could. Pressed into the dirt underneath, their colour nearly matching the dirt itself, were a hazy-grey pair of twisted spectacle frames.

"Harrison!" Felix called to the officer outside.

A shuffle of feet announced the man's arrival at the doorway. "Sir?"

Petters stood up and brushed the dirt from his knees. "Get the police surgeon here immediately." He held up the spectacles. "Bag these and take them back to the station."

"Yes, sir." The officer stepped forward to retrieve them.

Petters spied something yellowish white in the dirt beyond where the spectacles lay and he went to get a better look. What was it? Bird faeces perhaps? He peered closer then motioned to Harrison. "And this, get a sample of this."

"I will do, sir."

"Have Markham do a sweep of the area, I want to know who owns this building, what it's been used for, who has been here lately, cars in the area, you name it. Tell him to grab a couple of the afternoon shift officers to help him."

"You think it's the reporter's blood?" Harrison was on his knees gathering it up as best as he could.

"Could be. Or it could be nothing. I want this building

sealed—no ins or outs. Put someone on it immediately. We are going to have to go through it inch by inch."

"Got it."

The man left and Petters stared around the interior of the barn. Had someone dragged Jeremy Winston here and cut off his finger, ground his glasses into the dirt and then removed him again? Why? It seemed an inordinate amount of trouble to go to without having a motive. But who was he kidding, of course there was a motive. He just hadn't found it yet. And this irritated him no end.

"Yes, they are his." Lillie held the crushed spectacle frames in her hand, turning them over as she would a shell she had found at the beach. Carefully, methodically. She peered at them, and brushed her fingers over the bent wire frames. "He can't see a thing without them, you know." She placed them on Felix's desk and took a deep breath. "How much blood?"

"On the barn floor?" he asked, to which she nodded. "Quite a bit."

"So they've either killed him or moved him."

"Mm. It would seem so." Petters moved around the side of his desk and started to organize a bookcase that had been giving him angst, putting black spines with other black spines, then moving outwards based on the hue. First blue, then red, then green. Changing his mind, he transferred the green books to take the place of the blue books, realizing they were closer in saturation to the black than the blue books were. He stood back to survey his work.

"Felix!" Lillie snapped, obviously irritated with him, and he turned to give her his full attention.

"I've got officers interviewing every farmhouse within a twenty-mile radius." He assured her. "They had to have been driving to get him there, and then get him out of there again. I assure you, Lillie, someone will have seen something. We just need to find that person, and we will." He was giving her his focus, regardless of the spot of discolouration on his desk he had just noticed, and he had every intention of finding Jeremy Winston. "Trust me," he added, then surreptitiously rubbed at the spot with his shirt sleeve.

Lillie shot him a dissatisfied look. "I'm printing it. Everything about Jeremy's disappearance and the link to the deaths of Edwin Hastock and Andrew Baker."

Petters gave her a wary look. "We haven't formally established anything yet. Why would a newspaper reporter be tied up with a couple of Oxford students?"

"Well, that's the big question, isn't it?" Lillie stood up to signal the end of their conversation. "I have to get home, Felix. Nanny is heading out for the evening and I need to stop by the newspaper first. I've put together a crew of three investigative reporters who are combing absolutely every story we have covered in the past ten years."

Petters nodded his understanding. "You'll find it if it was a story he should have covered but didn't. No doubt he kept notes, files?"

Lillie frowned her frustration. "Yes," she agreed. "At least I hope he has. His office has been taken apart paper by paper."

"You'll find it if it's there," he reassured her, even though he was having doubts on absolutely everything. Without a thread, they had very little to go on. The blood on the floor of that abandoned barn meant Lillie's boss was in very serious trouble, if he was alive at all, which he was beginning to doubt.

HARRY

"Lillie should be here shortly," Harry assured the coxswain of the Oxford rowing team as he wandered to the sideboard to pour him a cup of tea from an unusually patterned Paragon tea set. It had been a wedding gift from his aunt in Scotland, a woman with horrific taste, and Harry half hoped the kitchen maid might be so inclined as to drop it en route to the sink. "She's usually very punctual," he continued, attempting to avert his eyes from the garishly designed cup as he handed it to Will Andrews. "Although I can just imagine what having a baby does to her daily routine."

They were comfortably seated in the large and airy drawing room at Tynesmore, Harry's ancestral home. A set of white doors were thrown open to the terrace and beyond it a herd of five horses grazed, an orchestra of swishing tails and muzzled sneezes. The room itself was garden-like. Harry had decorated it himself just before he had married Primrose, and with the exception of the argument with Rumple on whether or not the quarter sawn oak floors should be re-stained a dark ebony or a golden honey, the two of them had, for the most part, agreed on the overall aesthetic. It had taken a couple of trips to London, the two of them like an old married couple sorting bolts of fabric in the some of the finest shops in Knightsbridge, but eventually they had agreed on the fresh floral chintz that now graced the furniture and coordinated well with the soft green curtains.

Harry studied his guest. Will was the archetypical Oxford man. Tall, fair-haired, blue-eyed, self-confident. He had the build of a coxswain, a slight and narrow chest descending into an even narrower waist and muscular but lean thighs. The antithesis to his teammates, a coxswain needed to be slight. He wore a blazer over a faintly-checked cotton shirt and flicked his hair back as he sipped his tea—a move that irritated Harry mostly because he realized it was something he himself did and he thoroughly disliked a cliché.

Harry attempted small talk. "Disturbing news out of Italy this week," he started, lifting his teacup to his lips.

Will gave him a blank look.

Harry tried elaborating. "Imagine dissolving all political parties who *aren't* fascist." He hoped this would prompt some sort of response from the coxswain but the man hardly stirred. Was it even worth it to continue? "I do rather wonder what the future holds for the country."

Will nodded in a vague way while he glanced around the room. "I daresay," he responded, without a shred of understanding or interest.

Harry attempted another thread. "So—who do you think will win the Tour this year?"

Will perked up. At least they were on solid ground now. "Pelissier, I should think," the coxswain answered without hesitation. "He's in the best shape of his life and he's won every other major race this year."

Harry smiled at his own ability to find common ground with even the thickest of sportsmen. It was no wonder the man was still at Oxford—it was looking increasingly likely that he didn't possess the mental stamina to change a bike tyre much less obtain a degree. Just for fun, Harry engaged. "Presumably then the poor man will be exhausted." He knew nothing of cycling races and cared even less.

"When Desgrange wrote that he didn't have the ability to 'suffer' it was the spark, no doubt, that lit the fire. If there is one thing Henri doesn't like, it's being written off as a dilettante."

What *was* the man going on about?

Harry nodded as though he were interested and for amusement echoed the man's previous statement announcing his oblivion. "I daresay," Harry repeated.

Where was Lillie? He needed saving.

Will pointed out the doors, beyond the terrace, to the horses. "Quite the handsome breeding stock you've got."

Harry followed his line of vision. "Mm. Yes. Well, they certainly would be if any of them were sound. It's been a year of swollen tendons and bone chips." He sighed as the horses spooked at something and picked up a group trot to the far end of the field. "Odd that," he mused, studying their level movement. "Apparently they are only lame when I send them to the track and attempt to put a jockey on their backs. It does make one wonder if they aren't faking it all in order to get back to the grazing."

A clacking of shoes in the hallway outside the drawing room diverted their attention.

Rumple entered wearing an astonishing change of clothes from earlier that morning and Harry fought the urge to explode into laughter, the crowning piece being a plumed cavalier hat which he had cocked to one side and was now balancing precariously over his left ear.

Lillie breezed in behind him. "I'm so terribly sorry for being late," she apologized, shaking Will's hand. "Lillie Mead. I'm a friend of Harry's and a reporter for the *Oxford Daily Press*."

Harry could see Will visibly freeze at the mention of the

newspaper. He opened his mouth to reassure him but Lillie was already a step ahead of him.

"Anything you say today will be off the record—I'm not here in the capacity of a reporter."

Will nodded his understanding.

Lillie continued, discreetly pulling her notebook out of her shoulder bag. "How long have you been coxswain for Oxford?"

"Two years. Originally I wanted to be regular squad but I never had the physique to make it. I'm a little tall to be a coxswain but not tall nor strong enough to row. Which is fine with me, I like being where I am."

"And you knew Edwin Hastock?"

"Yes, of course. You mustn't know much about rowing, Miss Mead, if you think it's possible to have a team member, past or present, that I don't know."

His delivery irritated Harry. Were all Oxford boys this arrogant? Was he? He made a mental note to pay more attention.

"Lots of team events, I can imagine," Lillie answered, smiling deliberately.

Harry studied her carefully. She was wonderfully disarming, or certainly could be, when she wanted something.

"Yes, you could say that," Will answered. Another maddening flick of the hair.

"Of past and present squad members," she confirmed.

"Yes, if they are in town. But we often have a quite a good turnout."

"How often do you hold these gatherings, if that's the correct term for them." Another smile.

She was baiting him. Harry could see it as clearly as a car accident on an icy road. It was slow to start and one could clearly see the car about to make impact but the lead up was mesmerizing to watch.

"A few times a year."

"And do you have them in the same place all the time?"

"I think we are a bit more interesting than that, Miss Mead."
It was all but confirmed. Will Andrews was insufferable.

"I can imagine," Lillie responded airily. "Incidentally, did you know Andrew Baker? I've confirmed with the dean's office that he never formally rowed for Oxford, but there isn't a record of who practiced with the team. I thought you might be able to shed some light on it for me."

"I knew of him, yes. Mostly because of the cheating scandal he was caught in last year, but as far as I know he didn't practice regularly with the team. I mean, he might have been there a few times; I'm not always there early season when all the overly eager prospects come out. I wait until they die off and leave the core group."

"Could you elaborate on the cheating scandal?" Lillie asked.

"Oh, hardly anything noteworthy. Baker and a few others used a small underground outfit to complete a few papers for them—it happens more often than the university realizes. It blew over eventually."

"I see," Lillie said, noting it with a quick flick of her pen.

She switched back to the previous discussion. "Would these early-season rowers ever be at team gatherings? With the *past and present* rowers." Her enunciation went over his head. He may have been a confident man but he was nearly as stupid as the Tynesmore rooster who routinely left the hen house and forgot how to get back. Harry's groom was constantly finding the bird nestled under the straw in one of the mare's stalls. He'd nearly lost his life a year previous when he had bedded down with one particularly aggressive stallion so he supposed the damn bird was at least smart enough to choose the safer alternative. Which was more than could be said for Will who was quite easily wading into the netting Lillie had laid for him.

"More tea?" Harry asked, interrupting.

"Please." Will held out his cup as though Harry was his servant. Harry got up and retrieved it with a snap. "Yes, I suppose they might come out. They can be quite the social events and who doesn't like a good party?"

"Any idea if Andrew Baker knew Edwin Hastock? They were both from York originally."

"I would assume so, at least peripherally. But I can't confirm that I ever saw them in deep conversation."

Lillie agreed. "It's a pretty tightly-knit group, by the sounds of it. I can see it would be difficult for anyone in the rowing world at Oxford not to know another rower."

"Or Cambridge," Will added.

He nodded as Harry handed him back his full teacup, fighting the urge to tip it into the coxswain's lap.

"Oh?"

"Mm. We have a couple of practices together here during the season and they often reciprocate. We usually have a dinner afterwards, either there or here."

"I would have thought the two universities would be bitter rivals." Lillie said.

"In a regatta, yes of course, but not so much during the regular season." He took a sip of his tea. "We aren't that much different from one another, after all." He laughed. "A bunch of old boys looking to have a good time."

Was this *really* the best Oxford could do? Harry wondered. Sending these hedonists out into the world in the hopes they would represent England admirably? Or had he just become a mature old man in the time he had been away from university? He frowned and settled his eyes on his herd beyond the French doors. They had made their way to the far end of the field and a couple of them had collapsed onto the soil underneath an enormous oak tree, their legs folded like a couple of collapsible chairs. One of his young fillies had the most enormous belly, he noted with dissatisfaction. It would be nearly impossible to get her back into racing shape.

Harry brought his attention back to the room. Lillie was

keeping a neutral face but he knew that underneath the facade she would be about ready to pounce on this idiot. Had he really not realized what a fool he actually was?

"How about David Spool?" Lillie asked, gently placing her teacup on the table beside her chair.

Will raised his eyebrows. "What about him?"

"He was Edwin's roommate. Did you ever cross paths with him?"

"I try not to," Will answered, flippantly.

"Is that so? Why not?"

"He's a little strange, don't you think?" Will flipped the question back to her.

"I wasn't with him long enough to judge," she answered cooly.

Will flicked his hair back, again. Again it irritated Harry. "Well, anyway, he's an odd one—we didn't socialize much with him."

"Who is we?"

"Oh, you know," he said absently. "The boys."

"Odd how?" Lillie persisted and Harry nodded his encouragement.

"He just isn't like the rest of us. I half wondered if he shouldn't have stayed at Hanwell after he and his cronies finished their assignment there."

Lillie leaned forward. "I don't seem to be following you."

Will tipped his teacup and swallowed the last of the liquid. "He was part of the university's social directive to establish a therapeutic programme for the insane at Hanwell Asylum outside of London. You know how artists are—a little different from the rest of us."

"When was this?"

"Oh, some time ago; I can't really remember. Spool was there, as were a bunch of others. But he really took the whole project to heart and ran with it." He grimaced. "Imagine being someone who thrived on immersing with the insane. Makes one wonder somewhat about him, doesn't it?"

"I see." Lillie scribbled something into her notebook. She looked up and gave the coxswain a false smile, which Harry saw right through. "Well, I can't thank you enough for your time today." She remained seated—no doubt making her point that Will would be the one to be leaving Harry's home, not her.

Harry stood, revelling in the suggestion that the interview with this piece of fluff was finally over. "I'll just show you out, shall I?" he said, fighting the urge to beam.

22

DANIEL

"Lillie," he murmured, rolling her body towards him in the darkness.

"Mm," she responded sleepily, letting him pull her closer against his naked body. Reaching up, she circled two slender arms around his neck and buried her face into his skin. Then she did the same with her legs, wrapping them around his calves, and he felt them sear him. She was the loveliest creature, he thought contentedly, and he wanted to keep her entwined with his limbs forever. He found her mouth and kissed her gently at first, then with more urgency, feeling his whole body respond. He wrapped one long arm around the small of her back and moved her with him as though they were one instead of two.

Her bedroom was hot from the day and what little breeze there was barely picked at her gauzy drapes. It was past midnight and they had only just drifted off after settling Lola back into her crib. He half hoped they wouldn't sleep at all between her feedings, but judging from the dark circles under her eyes, he knew Lillie needed it. He regretted waking her now but he wanted her with him while he worked over his dilemma

—reviewing it and the options that had been presented to him. Not that she knew about any of it. She wasn't over his abandoning her in France, and since his clandestine return to Oxford she had alternated between being cold and distant and wildly passionate. He never quite knew what he was going to find when he came to her after dark. At least she had stopped scolding him about his presence there. They had settled into a routine whereby he would arrive after dark and leave before sunrise and if you asked him, he could continue doing it for all eternity if that was all she would give him.

Tonight she had been too tired to argue about anything and he had undressed her quickly and placed her between the sheets. Twice he had checked the doors to her cottage to ensure they were locked. He could hear her breathing change and he realized she had fallen back asleep on his chest. Her hair tickled his chin and he spiralled one dark lock around his forefinger. Would they find him here? He thought about it every minute. He had half decided not to come back to her but that in itself presented a dilemma. If they tracked Lillie to get to him and he wasn't in her life, then how would he know? If he was here, at least he could protect her and Lola from the people from his past. They were coming for him. After the carnage that had happened on his return to New York how could he possibly expect anything different.

But they didn't know about Lillie, not yet anyway. He exhaled and pulled her closer, listening for any unusual sound outside. For now, at least, everything was quiet.

23

LILLIE

Cornmarket Street was nearly empty.

The early morning air had a freshness to it and Lillie thought of Lola who she had left sleeping in the cottage with Daniel. She mentally counted the number of bottles she had left in the icebox. Were three enough? Nanny White had gone to her daughter's small farm in Elsford overnight and wasn't expected back until dinner time, and while Lillie had seen Daniel with Lola enough now to know he was as gentle and careful with her as she was, it was odd to actually leave her in his care entirely. She had given him a very brief lesson in diaper changing during the middle of the night when Lola had woken for her feed, and he had handled the baby with as much dexterity as she had seen him do with anything he touched. They should be fine, she reasoned. And anyway, she could hardly call Primrose and ask her to go to the cottage and take over from the assassin who was sleeping in her bed. She didn't plan to be gone long anyway.

She needed to check on the progress of the team she had assembled at the newspaper. They had been trying to find anything Jeremy might have been working on that would explain his disappearance, although so far they had come up empty-handed. It was the most frustrating type of search—they were actually looking for something that in all likelihood didn't exist.

She pushed through the front door of the newspaper, noting the absence of the receptionist. She checked her watch —the woman was late. She hurried past the desk and into the newsroom. There was a large, glassed office near the rear of the space and Lillie had commandeered it for her team the day Jeremy's finger had been sent to her. It was empty but for her one loyal assistant—a young man of twenty who had recently dropped out of university and come to work for them instead.

"Anything?" she asked him, as she moved into the room and pushed her shoulder bag into a chair.

He looked up at her and removed his glasses, rubbing at his eyes. Lillie wondered what time he had come in—or had he even left?

"Two things, although I'm not sure either of them are meaningful in any way." He got up and made his way to the other end of the long table where he had a small stack of newspapers that sat separate from the rest. "Neither of these stories were covered by us, and they probably should have been." He fanned the papers as though to make his point.

"Tell me."

"The first was a boating accident on the river two years back."

"In Oxford?"

"No, London. Putney area."

Lillie twirled a piece of hair around her finger. "Well, why would we cover it? We are a local paper and if it doesn't happen in Oxford, chances are we wouldn't give it precious print space."

"True, and I'd thought of that. But *this* accident involved a couple of students from the university. One was killed, a young

man by the name of Halliwell. The other one was never found."
He looked up at her and raised his glasses. "Presumably
drowned."

"Was there anything to suggest that perhaps it was more
than an accident?"

"Not really. They were out in a small boat late at night and
they were hit by a larger barge. Although it does seem rather
odd they couldn't manoeuvre a boat like that out of the way.
Even in the dark one could hardly miss a barge hurtling
towards you, I wouldn't think."

"Unless they were intoxicated." Lillie reasoned.

"I suppose so."

Lillie took the paper from him. It was the weekend edition
of a larger London paper and Lillie had always found their
reporting to be fairly competent and comprehensive. She
scanned the story, wondering if it had anything to do with
anything. Doubtful. "What was the second story you found?"

"I'm not sure on this one; it was a franchise equality march
in Oxford but this goes back a little while now." He raised his
teacup and took a long drink.

"Oh?"

"Apparently it erupted into some violence and the *Tribunal*
reported that there may have been a few injuries, possibly even
a death, although at the time of the story it was too early to
confirm."

"Any follow-up?"

"None."

Lillie gave a dissatisfied snort. Wasn't that always just the
way? A women's movement getting little to no real press even
when it resulted in personal injury. "Why don't you see if you
can get in touch with the reporter who wrote the story and ask
why they didn't follow it up with a later one. If only to make a
bloody point that what happens to women is just as important
as what happens to men. Honestly."

"Yes, of course."

Their discussion was interrupted by a screech of tyres in front of the newspaper building and Lillie hurried over to the window to see just the tail end of a car as it careened out of sight and around the corner. On the pavement by the front door lay a body in foetal position.

"What on earth is going on!" she exclaimed, running out of the room and through the newsroom to the exterior door of the newspaper office.

She flung it open in haste, hurrying down the three worn marble stairs that took her to street level. Although the body was still at least twenty feet from her, she recognized the clothing even before she recognized the man wearing them— brown tweed, now filthy and dusty, and an ivory dress shirt— and it was no wonder. She stared down at a face swollen and blood-soaked, eyes closed and puffy but facing skyward as though there might be something he wanted to see, could he but open them.

"Jeremy?" Lillie spoke to him, frantically falling to her knees beside him, but to little effect. He was unconscious, one hand wrapped in a filthy cloth, blood oozing through its thin fabric.

It was less than a minute before her assistant was at her side.

"I've called for the ambulance," he said to her, breathless. "It won't be long."

Lillie reached out thinking perhaps she could move Jeremy from his awkward position. He had one arm pushed at an unnatural angle underneath his body and it looked terribly uncomfortable.

"No, don't. You've no idea of the extent of his injuries. Leave him until the ambulance gets here." her assistant urged.

By the time they heard the ambulance's bell, a small crowd had begun to gather around the nearly lifeless body of the *Oxford Daily Press* chief. Gasps and sighs circulated through the onlookers as though they were watching a tightrope walker over Niagara Falls, and Lillie waved them away impatiently to make room for the great black hulk of the advancing ambulance. The attendants hopped out of the vehicle and brought a light stretcher over to where Lillie was kneeling beside Jeremy. He hadn't stirred and although he was breathing, it was barely discernible.

Once he was carefully loaded and the rear doors to the van were shut, Lillie burst into the tears she'd been holding back. If he lived, Jeremy Winston wouldn't ever be the same again.

24

LILLIE

"There's something in it, I'm sure of it." Harry sipped his tea later that evening at Lillie's cottage, his lithe, perfectly clothed legs stretched out before him while she fought back a yawn and shuffled the notes at her desk.

Lillie had returned home from the hospital at supper time to relieve Daniel and feed Lola—although neither of them had seemed to be in any hurry for her to come back. The two of them had been circling the garden, Daniel pushing the pram in search of peaches, or so he had said. When she'd asked him what for, he'd looked at her as though she were daft. *Well, dessert of course,* he'd answered, to which she'd promptly responded that he wouldn't be staying for dinner. He'd given her a look that suggested he knew exactly what she was going to say to him and, in fact, he had given her that ridiculous answer just to hear her response. Sometimes she wondered if he purposely liked to stir the pot with her.

Now she was looking for the papers she'd taken from the newspaper that morning and was having trouble keeping on thread after her day at the hospital. She was feeling slightly better about Jeremy's prognosis. While his injuries were mostly superficial, he'd also been diagnosed as having transient global amnesia, most likely brought on by the severe emotional and physical abuse of his kidnapping. It meant that when he would get his immediate memory back was anyone's guess. A poorly understood condition, it could be hours, or weeks, possibly even months, the doctors had explained to her. But at least he would live, the rest could come later. "Sure of what?" she asked Harry again.

"The cheating scandal, Lillie. Do try to pay better attention."

"Andrew Baker?"

"The armless chap, yes. I really don't think there was much in the Bath doctor's persona to suggest he might be doing all this killing. Therefore I'm on to the next of the dead. If it wasn't Edwin Hastock's past—poor dead girl in the river and all that—then perhaps it was Andrew Baker's."

"I see. It sounds terribly gruesome. Aha! Found them." Lillie held up a stack of papers in victory.

"Good girl. Now, should we perhaps try to understand what on earth that ghastly coxswain was talking about. A cheating scandal at Oxford would be quite embarrassing for the university."

"Harry, I hardly think it would be something to kill a student for! What sort of university do you think we attended, and how would this affect Edwin Hastock? Was he also cheating? Your imagination is running away with you."

"I'm simply saying we should investigate it. Perhaps it was something someone thought should have been reported in the newspaper and Jeremy didn't do it? A disgruntled student who didn't appreciate a ruffian like Baker stealing the limelight. It's hardly the Oxonian way, after all."

Lillie cocked one ear to the stairs, thinking she heard Lola. She fought the urge to run up and check on her for the hundredth time. Glancing at the clock she wondered how long

Harry planned to stay. Daniel often got there around ten and it was nearly nine thirty. Surely he would be back tonight even though it hadn't been all that long since he left. Should she tell Harry she needed a bath, and hope he took the hint?

"Well, I don't think we'd have much to go on. We can hardly ask Jeremy if he remembers anything about it, the doctors say whatever amnesia he is experiencing could be here for quite some time."

"Of course he remembers you though, dear girl. Incidentally, did the man not keep notes?"

"I doubt he kept notes on something he wasn't planning to write about. That's the whole bleeding problem, isn't it?" Lillie flopped down on the sofa across from Harry. "But you're right, it's worth looking into." She'd call on Petters in the morning and see where he was at with everything. "Why don't we pay the dean a visit tomorrow?" she suggested. "At least rule it out."

"Or in, my dear girl. Or in." Harry sighed, poured himself another cup of tea and settled in for the evening.

"*CHEATING*?" The Dean of Oxford University was a small man of nearly sixty with a hooked nose and protruding tufts of nose hair which matched his thick white eyebrows. "Oh, no, no, no. Certainly not." The man sat back in his leather desk chair and gave Lillie and Harry a stare which would have easily dislodged even the most distinguished guest.

They were seated in the dean's third floor office of New College, a handsome fourteenth-century building dripping in wisteria. Lillie looked out of the large leaded glass window to her left at the honeyed cloisters and expansive lawn, beyond which lay the walled gardens. She could understand his reticence. A bastion of architectural magnificence, the entire quadrangle of buildings seemed to, brick by limestone brick, hold its students and staff in the highest esteem. It was no wonder the dean seemed offended at the suggestion of something as unsavoury as cheating. It was as though she were accusing its founder, the revered William of Wykeham, of heresy.

"Of course it was never made public." Lillie thought about taking out her notebook and pen but decided against it. It would make him nervous if he thought she was recording the details of their meeting.

"I haven't the faintest idea what you are getting at, Miss Mead, but isn't it just like women to try to stir up trouble, especially these days."

The dean was a stalwart ivory tower dweller who had seen little of life outside the university, that much was glaringly obvious, but his comment struck a chord. Not only because it seemed to come out of nowhere and have no relevance to their conversation, but also because of the fashion in which it was pitched. Women's rights seemed to really bother the man, to the point that he wasn't able to hide his true feelings on the matter.

"These days?" she echoed, intentionally baiting him.

"Oh, you know, franchise equality and all that nonsense. All these young and irresponsible girls who think they should be allowed to vote. What do they *really* know of the world? Once they've attained some maturity, they'll get their opportunity. What more do they want? Honestly, clogging up the streets with their protests and taking over the newspapers with their rhetoric is hardly endearing or ladylike in any way." He waved his hands dismissively.

"I hardly think equality for all is 'rhetoric'."

Harry, who had been watching their exchange with amusement, piped in, "Which isn't really why we are here today." He firmly stared Lillie down. "There must be an outfit in town where one might go if they *were* to cheat. Not that there *has been* any cheating. Hypothetically speaking, of course." Harry uncrossed his legs and sat back in his chair. "Or possibly a disgruntled student who had been unseated as a result of Andrew Baker's impeccable scores?"

The dean looked increasingly uncomfortable and began to shift around in his seat. "You are discussing the student who was murdered now?"

"Mm." Harry nodded.

"You think he may have been murdered by a disgruntled student? How preposterous!"

"Perhaps." Harry took a pale-green sterling and enamel cigarette case out of his pocket and offered one to the dean but the man shook his head. Harry lit up anyway, making smoke rings above their heads. "But it *is* a theory."

"What about the other boy who was also murdered in Henley? Hastock. Are you suggesting that he was also cheating?" The dean looked surprised at the direction the conversation had taken.

"If I could find the organization who might have helped Baker obtain the information he used to cheat, then I could track down whether or not Hastock was involved, yes." Harry stubbed his cigarette out, half smoked, into a small pewter ashtray on the table between his chair and Lillie's. She was increasingly sure that Harry only smoked in order to show off the tricks he could do. He was the least committed smoker she'd ever met.

"I've no idea where one would look for an organization as morally corrupt as the one to which you are referring. As far as I know, there has been no cheating at Oxford University."

"I see." Harry looked tremendously disappointed. No doubt he was hoping his presence as an alumnus would have catapulted him into the inner circle.

Lillie had had nearly enough of the dancing around. "Although that's not strictly true now, is it? When I attended not long ago there were at least three incidents of cheating that were brought to the dean's attention."

"I have no doubt, Miss Mead, that if you check the records you will find no such occurrences."

I don't doubt that, Harry grumbled, barely audible under his breath.

"Right." Lillie stood up. She'd had just about enough of the man and they were hardly getting anywhere. "Thank you for your time." She gathered up her bag, while Harry scrambled to follow suit.

When they had emerged into the hallway outside the dean's office, Harry put one hand on Lillie's arm. "Slow down, why didn't you continue with your questioning? You let him off the hook."

"I don't believe any of this has to do with cheating on exams, Harry. Even if Baker cheated, so what? It doesn't mean Hastock did. If there was a disgruntled student wanting to blow it open then why wouldn't he just do that? He wouldn't kill two people and then not say why."

"Maybe he tried and was thwarted. You saw the dean; he won't accept even a whisper of an accusation. Perhaps he went to the newspaper and Jeremy refused to print anything so he had no choice but to become a vigilante."

"And a murderer? It's a stretch, Harry."

"So why is the dean so jumpy?"

They had reached the main doors to the building and the two of them emerged into the July sunshine and crossed the lawn.

"Well, that's the big question now, isn't it? But I will say this, he certainly doesn't appreciate the franchise equality movement or the way it's disrupted college life."

"I'm sure you could say that for a lot of people though," Harry put in.

"Yes, I suppose so. But the dean was different. I think there's more to him than meets the eye, Harry."

"That may be, but I still plan to ask around about the

cheating before we rule it out." They had reached the main road and Lillie veered left to head towards the newspaper office.

"You do that," she agreed. "And I'll go and pull what I can on all the franchise rallies over the past few years. But where we really need to get to is Hanwell."

Harry looked at her as though he'd just eaten a sour cherry. "The insane asylum?"

"That's correct. Remember the coxswain said David Spool headed up an initiative there?"

"What are you expecting to find?" Harry asked.

"I've no idea but while we are following up on car accidents, cheating and franchise rallies, we may as well research David Spool as well."

"I see." Harry glanced around the busy street as though he were expecting a stranger's car to stop any minute and pick him up. "I'm busy that day," he concluded.

"I haven't told you the day, Harry." Lillie folded her arms in front of her. "And anyway, it's tomorrow and Primrose said you've got nothing on."

"Well that is just preposterous, how does she know everything I've got going on?" he huffed. "I've just started back with the golfing."

"Oh, have you? And what was your last score?"

"Well, I can't remember now."

"You are not being admitted, Harry. I just need some company."

"Take Felix."

"He's busy following up on Jeremy's case. He can't possibly go running around the country chasing up leads. That's my job. And you, my friend, are up."

25

"They were geraniums, I believe."

She looked as though she couldn't really remember and she scrunched her eyes, the way she'd used to do when she was alive—when she would find herself in deep thought—then she shook her head, silently, to disagree.

"They were, I'm sure of it."

"Tobacco flowers," she asserted, as though her memory was perfect now she had really given it some deep thought.

"Well anyway, they were pink."

"And white," she added. She always was the most precise girl.

"If you insist." The last thing they needed was a battle. It was better to let her win.

They had only seen them in passing that evening two years ago so how were either of them to really remember? The rest of that fateful evening had given them enough to remember—the flowers, by contrast, had faded far into the distant background. What colour they had been then, as they decorated the limestone walls of an Oxford college, was hardly important now. Regardless of how beautiful they had both thought them at the time, what had come to pass a mere few hours after they had admired them still broke both their hearts.

They had reached the front door of the pub and they hesitated for just a moment before the door was opened by a raucous group of young men and women who flooded out into the summer sunlight and dispersed in a fit of laugher and good-byes, the scent of beer and sweat on the air.

She shivered and they both fought to suppress the memories of two years ago.

"There isn't any point in waiting."

She nodded her understanding.

"Right. So here we go." Looking back at her standing there, hesitantly reliving her horror, was heart-wrenching.

They entered the darkened room and headed past sticky tables and over the worn carpeting to a bar in need of revarnishing.

The man behind the counter barely gave them a glance while they both seethed.

"A pint, please." Giving the barman an order made them look like they were just normal paying customers. It had been years, after all, he would hardly remember them. One of them he couldn't see anyway.

He nodded his affirmation and set to pouring the pint. A burley man with an untrimmed beard he didn't look much different than he had all that time ago. Still unkempt, still a man who appeared not to feel responsible for his actions, or lack of them. Still a disgusting waste of air and space.

"Been busy?" Making small talk brought their anxiety down.

"Better now I've got the outdoor area open." The man pointed to a rear door that was propped open, allowing a stream of sunlight to illuminate the filth on the floor. They could just see a couple of mismatched tables, also dirty, which sat empty. "It's still early," he finished, as though he were reading their minds.

They both fought the urge to roll their eyes, not that he would have seen hers. It *was* still early—that was the plan, wasn't it? To come in when there wasn't much chance of being disturbed. The large group that had just left had caused them some concern, the last thing they needed was to be seen, but the place was relatively empty now. The one lone occupied table had an older gentlemen who was now gingerly rising from his seat to pay his bill.

They surveyed their surroundings while the barman tended to the old man, reflecting on the delicious lack of patrons and the location of the kitchen. If they ordered food, eventually he would either have to go back there and make it himself or have the chef do it. Because it wasn't quite lunchtime, chances were the chef wouldn't be in yet.

"I'll have the bangers and mash, if possible?" It was worth a shot.

"Sure can." The barman lumbered over to his pad of paper by the bar, scribbled something on it and headed towards the kitchen. They could hardly have asked for better turn of events.

They were off their barstools with the speed of a couple of cheetahs having found a lame antelope and everything happened as though it were a perfectly choreographed ballet with them as the lead. The knife had been tucked neatly under the sleeve of a coat and it glinted briefly as it was pulled from its hiding spot. Having no idea about what was coming next, the barman had advanced into an empty kitchen to get busy preparing the off-hour meal. What he didn't see was the short blade, brandished as though it were a sword and its wielder a knight. When it was driven with skill and precision between the shoulder blades with a swift upper cut into the heart, the man simply gurgled his dismay and fell forward onto the floor with a clatter, bringing down a pile of pots with him. It hardly mattered about the noise, there wasn't a soul around to hear it and the timing couldn't have been any more perfect.

Taking the man's ear was the most rewarding of all. It fell into their hands with relatively little effort, just like all the rest of the pieces they had gathered. A head for the mastermind, an arm for the first blow, a finger for the one who failed to write it, an ear for a man who pretended he couldn't hear it. They were amassing quite a collection.

The hot July sun shone on their backs as they exited the pub and made their way down the street with a skip in their step. It was cause for a celebration—a new dress perhaps? One that didn't need to be lengthened this time and from a shop where the salesperson didn't gawk.

Yes, they deserved it.

26

SUPERINTENDENT FELIX PETTERS

D avid Spool looked up from his book with surprise. The Bodleian Library, where he now sat at a large wooden table with space for eight, was quiet that morning. With most students on summer break, and those that weren't choosing to be outside, Spool likely thought he wouldn't be disturbed.

Felix Petters hadn't given him any warning that he would be meeting with him, which was just as he had planned it. In a policeman's experience, surprise could often be a formidable weapon. Not that he really thought Spool was hiding anything from their last meeting, but Felix liked to catch people off guard. He pulled out a seat across from Spool, removing a handkerchief from his pocket and giving the entire thing a good wipe down. When he was satisfied with its overall cleanliness, he sat down, careful not to place his hands directly on the table, and smiled at the student.

"Forgive my intrusion," he started politely.

Spool closed the book he was reading and Petters glanced at the author. Hegel. He had once tried reading the German's works himself, to no avail. He himself would have been glad for the interruption, but he wasn't so sure about Spool.

"Not at all," Spool answered.

Petter's pulled a photograph out of his pocket and lay it on the table. It was meant to shock, certainly, but Spool barely flinched.

"Who is this?" he asked.

Granted the police photographer wasn't the best they'd ever had, and nor was the condition of the body when they'd found it the previous evening, but one should have been able to identify the man if one knew him. They'd cleaned the blood off the deceased's face as best they could for the photograph.

"I wondered if you could tell me." Petters was purposefully elusive, watching Spool's face try to work it out.

"I've no idea, superintendent." He leaned over the photograph to get a better look. "Should I know?" His raised eyes held a blank expression. If he knew, he was certainly giving a laudable performance.

"No, not necessarily. It's a murder victim, found yesterday in an Oxford pub not far from one of the colleges."

"Most pubs in Oxford are near some college though, aren't they," Spool clarified. "Which pub?"

"The King's Arms," Petters answered, searching for some recognition. He was rewarded with another blank stare.

"I don't frequent many pubs, superintendent. I'm sorry, I don't know it. Is this somehow related to the Hastock and Baker murders? Is that why you are here?"

Petter's thought of the missing ear. Was it related? He certainly believed so. Body parts were piling up at a rapid pace.

"Can you tell me what you did during your semester at Hanwell Asylum?" He had reviewed Lillie's notes from her conversation with the coxswain a few days previous and he wanted all bases covered.

Spool looked confused at the sudden change of topic, or perhaps it was the question. "In what way?" he asked.

"Why you were there, generally. Was it your initiative? Or was it your department's initiative?"

"It was a collaborative approach, really. The university is often involved in social outreach programmes and their directive was multifaceted. It wasn't a very long programme and there have been a few others since. Would you like to hear about those as well?"

Petters studied the man. He wasn't as strange as the coxswain had suggested, at least Petters didn't think him so, and he was exceedingly smart. If there *was* something David Spool was hiding, it was doubtful Petters would find it easily.

"Not at the moment, no. I thank you for your time and I'm terribly sorry for interrupting your work."

Petters stood and smiled down at Edwin Hastock's roommate. "Incidentally, have there been any further letters sent to Edwin this summer?"

"Not that I've seen, no." Spool looked as though he had more to say on the matter but chose instead to remain quiet.

"Good day, Mr Spool."

Felix made his way out of the gloomy library into the sunshine and started his walk to the hospital to check in on Jeremy Winston. With any luck he would remember more today than he had the previous day.

"I'M TELLING YOU, young man, I know what I saw." The old woman was as diminutive in stature as she was substantial in personality. She shifted in her seat and crossed two thick ankles illuminating a long run on one side of her hosiery. Petters avoided looking at it by glancing out of the police station window.

Coming into the station on her own accord after a local plea by his constabulary for witnesses, she was the fourth witness Petters had interviewed since coming back from the hospital and each one of them had a slightly different description of the person or persons they'd seen leaving the pub after the latest murder. A couple of students had said they were quite drunk already but they'd seen a homeless man in a dark, flannel overcoat leaving the pub shortly before noon. A bricklayer had only seen the shoes of a person at approximately the same time but he'd swear on his mother's grave they were a burnished-brown lace-up variety, men's, well-polished. So hardly those of a homeless man, Petters had concluded. And now there was this woman who probably couldn't see past the end of her nose, sputtering something completely different again.

"One woman, tall and slim, leaving the pub at a quarter to noon." The old woman huffed and crossed her arms over her cardiganed bosom. Underneath it she wore a patterned blouse with miniature cherries on it that looked as though it belonged on a girl of ten, an interesting choice for a woman of eighty. "She was muttering to herself as if she were crackers." She waved a hand towards Jeremiah who was quietly sitting in one corner of the reception trying to mind his own business. Petters noticed the boy was failing miserably to fight back a creeping smile as he peered underneath his chair for his badger.

The woman continued, undeterred. "There wasn't a soul around and yet she seemed to be quite content having a conversation with no one in particular." She peered around her at the police office reception area and frowned at the Art Deco counter. "God awful, that." She lifted her cane and stabbed at the air in its general direction. Petters could hardly disagree, he too disliked the black, curved furniture. It was as sinister as a mobster's car.

Petters sighed. "Anything else you might be able to tell me about her?" he asked.

The woman looked up at the ceiling as though she could

pluck an answer from it, her rheumy eyes travelling back and forth along its coffers. "Had this straight hair, like a curtain almost, you know—hung as perfect as a doll's hair."

Petters scribbled that down. "Anything else? Size?"

"Size of the doll?" The woman looked confused.

"No, ma'am, I was wondering about the size of the person with the doll-type hair."

"Well she wasn't going to make the Royal Ballet, I can tell you that with certainty. Must've been a farmhand's daughter to have legs like that. I wouldn't doubt if she's from East Anglia, they grow them big there. If I were you, young man, I'd be starting there first."

In all of East Anglia? Was she serious? Petters imagined himself traipsing from farm to farm looking for a tall woman with hair like a curtain. "Yes, right. Well, I can't thank you enough for coming in." Maybe there was something in it but Petters was having a hard time imagining their killer would be female. The severed head seemed a bit gruesome, not to mention physically difficult for a woman to manage. And whoever had amputated Andrew Baker's arm and kidnapped Jeremy Winston would have had to have some serious physical strength.

When the woman had gone Petters opened his file and looked again at their photos of the crime scene. He pulled out one particular photo of the bartender, face down, and studied the entry wound on his back. A shorter killer would mean the wound would aim upwards and it would likely be messier having not had height for an advantage. A taller person would aim downwards, resulting in a neater wound. This one was nearly straight in. Medium height for a man, tall for a woman. It fit.

"It's probably a wig," Jeremiah piped up from the other side of the room. He had their now-healed badger on a home-made leash and harness and the animal was sniffing around the floorboards looking for a miraculous escape route. It was astonishing he'd never bitten the boy. "In my experience, if hair looks fake it probably is."

Petters smiled to himself, the boy was only fourteen. How much experience could he possibly have in his short life? "Which would mean this woman could be changing her wig..." he agreed, while scratching at his chin. It made things more complicated, assuming she was actually who they were looking for.

Jeremiah adjusted the badger's leash and gave him something to nibble on from his pocket. "And the killer knew where to aim, don't forget that."

Petters nodded. "Straight for the heart." Unless they were just lucky?

"Yes. Which goes back to my original theory of someone having some medical training."

Petters thought of Flora Stewart's brother, the doctor. Lillie didn't really believe he had anything to do with it and he tended to find that Lillie was a good enough judge of character to rule suspects out. But still, he shouldn't overlook his own training to follow up on each and every lead. Even if they did come from a fourteen-year-old boy.

"Except there's this, young man. The first two murders were Oxford students. This one is a pub worker. What are the chances they are even connected?"

"The missing ear, obviously," Jeremiah retorted matter-of-factly. "And the fact that the newspaper head was kidnapped and also suffered a missing body part."

"Right." Petters stood up to head to his office. He had a lot of work to do. "Are you taking that animal for a walk, or not?"

27

LILLIE

"I don't think I can actually go *in*," Harry said, hesitating at the large set of closed iron gates which were laboriously hung on an enormous stone archway, beyond which lay the extensive Victorian labyrinth of the Hanwell Insane Asylum. He peered through the grills at the steeple in the near distance at the end of the main gravel drive. The church was flanked on either side by identical panopticon buildings to which were attached long slim structures, four storeys in height, stretching their imposing stone bodies towards a rickety fire escape, and a series of parched vegetable gardens to the east with a cluster of low-lying cottages to the west. English ivy had overtaken the top half of the archway and what would have looked like a miniature version of the Arc de Triomphe looked instead like its much poorer, awkwardly-bearded cousin. In either direction of the gate extended a long, bleached brick wall culminating in twin guard buildings. All along the wall were small cutouts at regular intervals where the wardens could watch the goings on outside the asylum walls.

"Don't be silly," Lillie scolded, looking at the behemoth

before them and noting she could hardly blame him but she wasn't about to let on. "We've just come all this way. What could possibly be so terrifying now?" She glanced about her in order to make her point—to both of them.

It was an impeccable day, where the sky had turned a pale powder-blue in the heat, as though it, too, was parched by the sun. Hanwell was situated a mere eight miles from central London and had a handsome nesting of trees both left and right. The River Brent wound to the rear of the site—providing all the water the nearly eighty acres of Thames Valley asylum grounds needed for its patients and staff to be self-sufficient. It was a staggeringly enormous complex—throwing open its doors to the insane in 1831, and it had done nothing but grow in size since. In spite of it all though, the entire place gave her an eerie feeling, regardless of the sun's determination to wipe it away.

"I'm hardly being 'silly'," Harry replied, running a hand over his thick blonde hair as though he didn't know what to do with it. "It's a smashing day, I'll just take a stroll while you head on inside and find out what you can from their records department."

Lillie stopped hard in her tracks and glared at him. "What are you afraid of? Lunatics? Getting locked inside?" She pointed to the open field beyond the gates where a couple of patients wandered, composed though seemingly confused. "Look. It isn't a jail. Those men are outside enjoying the weather."

Harry nodded his chin towards a guard who stood at the edge of the field, rifle slung over one shoulder, while he smoked a cigarette, as though to make his silent point that he was relaxed enough to smoke and kill without remorse if he needed to.

"I need you to come in with me, Harry. You might not actually realize this, being who you are, but going in alone, as a woman, it is very likely I will be easily dismissed."

"You don't understand," he continued to plead. "I've always had this ghastly sensation when I arrive at an unsavoury place or a destitute circumstance that perhaps I could have quite easily ended up there...had I not been...oh I don't know, *lucky*, I suppose."

"How so?" Lillie asked, studying her friend and realizing there was still so much she didn't know about him.

"Well," he continued. "If I wasn't born Harry Green and instead I was born John Smith—and perhaps then I didn't have all the advantages I've had or the family I've had or its resources—you see what I mean."

"You mean you don't actually believe in the divine right of kings after all?" Lillie joked.

Harry remained pensive. "It doesn't make me feel good, going in there." He pointed through the gates.

"Nor I." Lillie agreed. "But I need you with me."

Harry nodded, summoning up his courage.

Lillie gave the guard who had been studying their exchange a wave and he sauntered his way over towards the gates.

"Lillie Mead to see Administrator Harris. He's expecting me."

The guard nodded his assent, unlocking the gate and swinging it inwards to admit them. "Down the gravel road and first building on your left." He pointed toward one of the panopticons and they moved slowly down the road together as though they were making tracks through quicksand.

Entering the building they spied the administrative office and made their way towards it, passing a waiting area sparsely populated with a couple of unforgiving wooden benches and two matching coat racks.

"I see they haven't wasted the decorating allowance, anyway," Harry whispered.

"Miss Lillie Mead to see Administrator Harris." Lillie smiled at the receptionist.

With a wooden nod that barely moved the woman's head, they were shown into a large circular office with windows that looked out and over the front lawns. Lillie noted the same patients they had recently passed still lingering confusedly on the grass, as though they were having difficulty finding their way back.

Harris was an overly large man who looked as though he would have been far more at home manning a prison than a hospital. When he stood to shake their hands Harry looked childlike by comparison.

"Good morning, Miss Mead, and Mr—"

"Green," Harry confirmed. "Harry Green."

"Welcome to our asylum," Harris said, taking his seat. "I gather from your initial correspondence that you have some inquiries about our work programme here in the asylum."

"Yes. I understand Oxford sent a group of students here some time ago to help put together a programme for your patients?" Lillie opened her shoulder bag and removed her notebook and a pen.

"That's correct. It was a quite an undertaking. Initially we had conceptualized that they would just help us with one or two areas—gardening perhaps, or culinary pursuits—we have an exceptional kitchen facility. Impeccably designed by Hutchinson and Wilkins, do you know them?"

"I don't, actually." Lillie endeavoured to keep him on point. "But they expanded their assignment, did they?"

"Mm, yes. Forgive me, would either of you like some tea," he digressed.

"No, thank you," Lillie nearly snapped. The entire place was beginning to get to her. She could hear the faint but unmistakable sound of wailing from somewhere deep within the recesses of the building's corridors which Administrator Harris pointedly ignored. Even in the heat of the day, Harry shivered beside her. "With regards to their assignment, it's my understanding the Oxford contingent also did some work in the medical facility, is this correct?"

"Ah, yes. A bit of a pet project of ours." Harris smiled, as though he had just personally birthed his first child.

"Oh?"

"We have an exceptional clinic in ward seven. Originally it started as a bit of a lab, really. We studied all sorts of animal parts, and some human. We have an arrangement with the London City Morgue—they send us parts when they no longer need them."

"Human parts?"

"Yes."

"Presumably the next of kin would like the parts of their loved ones, would they not?" Harry frowned at the administrator and Lillie noticed her friend had begun to sweat across his brow.

"Unclaimed bodies. I should have clarified," the administrator added, as though that somehow made it better. "Probably homeless. Street people and the like, no doubt."

"I see." Lillie felt a faint disgust at the whole scenario. The medically insane studying body parts of recently deceased individuals. It was hardly rehabilitational, was it? Gruesome, more like.

"In the name of art, of course," he added, reading the disapproval on her face. "The entire programme is based on the masters; Da Vinci to be specific." He raised his nose.

"Da Vinci," Lillie stated flatly, wondering what on earth the man was yammering on about.

"Yes, true anatomic correctness on the canvas must come from an in-depth study of form. One must peel back the layers, or the skin in this case, in order to understand muscle tone, the sinews for example, the fat, where the bone meets, a joint—"

Harry stopped him, turning nearly green. "Uh, yes, I think we are getting your meaning."

"Yes, well," Harris clipped, realizing he was indeed losing his audience. "We take our art programme very seriously. It is overseen by Oxford University and our curriculum is rigorously paralleled to theirs. The psychology department has been a staunch supporter of lunacy rehabilitation and has written extensively on our project here. Did you see the latest copy of the *British Medical Journal*? The university has just had a paper featured: 'The Resurgence of the Mind: A Study in Leisure and Lunacy'."

"I did rather miss it, I'm afraid." Harry shifted in his seat, turning to Lillie. "It must have been lost under a stack of racing papers." He raised his eyes to the ceiling.

"Do you have a list of the Oxford students who helped set up the programme here at Hanwell?" Lillie wanted not only confirmation of David Spool's attendance but of anyone else who might be associated with him.

"I suppose I must; I'll have to have a look through the files. To tell you the truth, I supposed you had come here today to view the facility and cover our work and recreational programmes in your newspaper. We have an extensive gardening programme as well if you would like more information on that? And the training we have undergone over the past year in the kitchen has been tremendous."

Lillie thought with nausea about the severed body parts and their victims, to say nothing of Jeremy Winston's disappearance. The very last thing she wanted to discuss was how to grow vegetables.

"While that is very interesting, we are mainly here to fully understand how you instituted the art programme here at Hanwell. And specifically, just who was part of that undertaking."

"Yes, of course, of course. I'll have the files pulled now. Patricia!" He hollered through the closed door, startling both of them. Harry winced his immediate disapproval. A woman who must have been listening at the door, if her promptness was anything to go by, appeared nearly immediately. "Ah good, please pull anything we have relating to our anatomical art programme, specifically who was here on-site for that two-week trial." When his assistant had gone, he turned to them and said, "Now, how about a little tour? A story in your newspaper would be appreciated, Miss Mead. One can never seem to have enough funding. As the saying goes, the squeaky wheel gets the grease."

Harry winced his displeasure but Lillie didn't see they had much choice. They had to wait for the files anyway and the sooner they had the man on side, the better.

"I should like nothing better," she lied, giving Harry a sideways wink.

28

"You'll have to let it down, there's no way around it."

She flicked back her cinnamon hair and set to work studying the tips of her fingernails as she sat perched on the edge of the dressing room chair. She'd always hated the white flecks in them and she stared hard at them as though she might will them away.

The reflection in the dressing room mirror only showed one of them, which was disturbingly perplexing the first time it had happened, but now they were used to it and didn't give it another thought.

"It shouldn't be very difficult though." They were constantly having to alter things, this would be no different.

The two of them together studied the hem line of the tweed skirt. They were always partners in everything.

"The pleats make it challenging," she concluded with dissatisfaction, sitting back up. "I still think you should consider something more feminine. That coral-coloured one was lovely, and if you wear it with that tie-blouse you bought last month it'll show more of a waistline on you. Why do you always go for the dowdy styles?"

She was absolutely right, of course, but it was more about not attracting attention to themselves now than it was about fashion. Perhaps they were being a little too careful. With three dead men in the bank and one terrified reporter in the hospital they could afford to live a little, couldn't they?

"Fine then. Go and get the coral one for me to try."

She hopped up and clapped her hands like a child. Pleasing her was the best feeling in the world.

The saleslady came to the door of the changing room and called through it. "Were you needing something else?" She tapped at the door a little too insistently and they reluctantly opened it for her. "Oh! I just heard voices and I thought someone was in here with you."

There was, of course.

"I was just talking to myself. I'd like to try on the coral skirt, the one near the front window, if possible."

The saleslady barely hid her surprise, her pancake make-up creasing unattractively into the lines above her raised eyebrows. "I'm...well, I'm not sure we have it in your size."

"Is that so? Well perhaps you might have a look."

The woman stubbornly stood her ground. "I just don't know if it would be the most flattering style on you."

"I daresay I should be the judge of that, don't you agree?"

They both felt the anger prickle their skin. There was a defiant flick of cinnamon hair and the hazel eyes hardened. Neither of them appreciated this smug righteousness they'd had to become so used to. The woman's lipstick ran into the cracks around her mouth as she pursed it and engaged them in a stare down. Which, of course, just made them want the coral dress even more.

"Will you fetch it? Or shall I?" It was intentionally derogatory but they'd really had enough.

The saleslady stood her ground, the ugliness of her opinions written all over her face. There was nothing as unattractive as narrow-mindedness. *"It won't fit,"* she enunciated, as though they were imbeciles.

Well, that wasn't it at all now, was it? It wasn't about the size or the colour or the style. It was about that fact that this horrible woman didn't want her clothes on one of them. That was the real crux of the whole thing.

She turned to leave the dressing room and both of them imagined the satisfaction they might have of assaulting her as she retreated. When she was gone, they looked at one another and smiled. It was a look they'd shared often over the years— camaraderie in larceny.

"Leave the tweed," she said with finality, her hazel eyes slit in a way that spoke more of her state of mind than any words could. She'd had enough.

"Of course. It just won't do now."

The saleslady was at the counter when they emerged from the dressing room and headed towards the front door. They breezed past as though she wasn't worthy of their considera-tion. The coral skirt in question was adorning a mannequin by the front door, her long hands and slender arms twisted in a way no woman's ever were, her head cocked to one side as though she were being idiotically coy.

It happened in a flash—one of them, and neither would remember which later, punched the mannequin squarely in the face knocking her off her base and sending her tumbling to the floor with a clatter. The other one crouched over her and unzipped the skirt, pulling it down and over her legs, careful not to rip the fabric. The last thing they needed was to do more alterations than were strictly necessary.

"Stop!" the saleslady cried. "What are you *doing?*" She was in a flutter of excitement as she put down whatever she was working on and rushed out from behind the counter.

The cinnamon hair glowed nearly amber in the light from the shop windows as she held the skirt up over her head, as though it were a trophy and she had just been crowned the heavyweight champion of the world.

The two of them exploded into fits of laughter as the door to the shop closed behind them and they skipped off down the street with a flash of coral.

29

HARRY

"Sir?"

Theodore Rumple stood on the threshold between the Tynesmore drawing room and the flagstone patio where Harry had decided to take an afternoon nap upon their return from Hanwell Insane Asylum.

Harry opened one eye and lazily studied his manservant, what *was* he wearing? Was that a violet cummerbund? "What time is it, Rumple?"

"Nearly six o'clock, sir, and I've really got to get set up for dinner; Miss Mead and her entourage should be here shortly."

"You make her sound as though she is a French politician at Versailles. It's only a baby, Rumple." He caught a glimpse of pure affection on Rumple's face. It was the same look he saw on Primrose's every time she was with Lola. Perhaps they should consider adopting, after all. It seemed as though their house needed a baby and the foals that Harry continued to buy year after year weren't really doing the trick. He frowned, thinking about the portly little two-year-old he'd hoped would start next year at Cheltenham but had instead developed a hiccup in his giddy-up. The veterinarian had diagnosed a bone chip but where the pesky little bit of ivory was floating around in his right front leg was anyone's guess. In all likelihood the handsome chestnut would become another field ornament to add to his already hefty collection.

"She is bringing that superintendent and his boy. I do really think you might consider getting up, sir. If you still wish to dine outside I'll need the seating you are lying on."

Harry stretched and reluctantly sat up. They were having dinner ridiculously early in order to accommodate Lola's evening schedule, which was fine with him but he really would have liked a bit of a longer snooze. "I've had a traumatic day, Rumple, you might be a little more sensitive to my predicament." Harry shuddered, thinking of the wails echoing off the corridors at the asylum and wondered if he would ever get them out of his head.

The director had taken him and Lillie on the most atrocious tour while they had waited for the documentation they'd requested. It was all damp stone and hollow-eyed patients, misery and misfortune. The medical rooms had the most grisly smell, not to mention jar upon jar of unrecognizable body parts soaking in formaldehyde. Were they animal or human? Harry had wondered. If one weren't insane to begin with, they would certainly become so fairly quickly there.

"You look like a barman, Rumple." Harry took in the leather arm bands. "For gangsters," he added. "Do you plan to change before our guests arrive?"

His manservant looked confused, staring down at his white, ankle-length apron which he wore over a button-up black leather vest. "No." He gave Harry a look to suggest he didn't appreciate his choice of clothing being questioned at this late hour.

"Your choice, as always, my good man. I'll just run up and bathe then, shall I?"

"Very good, sir. I'll have drinks served at six thirty on this terrace. Do hurry back."

Harry wondered briefly on his way back into the house and up the grand staircase just who was employed by who.

BY SIX FORTY-FIVE when Harry and returned, bathed, dressed and shaved, the terrace at Tynesmore had been transformed into a summer wonderland of lanterns, flowing floral tablecloths and great bursting silver bowls of flowers. The estate had a hothouse that all winter produced some of the finest buds, which the gardeners then painstakingly moved outside and planted all around the estate in the summer months. Huge, open peonies in light and dark pinks were the result, along with white lavender, any colour or variety of rose you could dream up and a plethora of lilies. Tonight Rumple had chosen the peonies and had them coordinated in separated bowls of pastels or hot pinks, their sterling silver urns polished to perfection.

Lillie and Lola had already arrived and Primrose hadn't wasted any time gathering the baby into her arms, and Felix Petters, as was customary with his regimented personality, had shown up five minutes early. Harry, by contrast, was late as usual while Jeremiah, on the other hand, was conspicuously absent.

"Is your young man not with us tonight?" Harry asked Petters, as the man brushed ants off the table cloth, one by one, careful not to injure or maim any of them. "They open the peonies," Harry explained, watching a steady march of six-legged creatures as they made their escape, winding around the wine goblet stems to freedom. Perhaps Rumple might have been better off choosing the lilies, he thought.

"Oh yes, he wouldn't miss it. He's already been invited to the kitchen, however, so I'm not sure how much of him we'll see before dinner."

"Hardly his fault, I'm sure." Harry's cook loved any customer who appreciated the fruits of her toiling efforts and had no doubt set him up at the large oak work table below the main floor to ooh and ahh her creations for the evening. "Come sit, superintendent. Leave those, they'll be gone shortly of their own accord."

"Lil!" Harry called over his shoulder. "Leave that darling baby for a moment with Primrose and come, let's discuss our day at that ghastly asylum." He gave Petters a stern look. "I shan't be returning in case you have any clandestine ideas of who needs to go in and investigate further."

"That bad?" Petters asked, as Rumple brought him a very large gin and tonic. "I don't actually..." he called to his retreating back.

He was going to say drink, Harry surmised, but Rumple had floated off back out of earshot in the direction of his makeshift bar, a nearly priceless Dutch Louis XVI sideboard he'd hauled outside, as though he were a bee returning to the hive. His long apron swished sideways as he walked, its open back giving them a snippet view of his purple cummerbund, and Harry watched with amusement, hoping he wouldn't trip on it.

"If there is one thing about Rumple, superintendent, it's when he gets his mind on a role he sticks with it. Tonight it's barman. Bottoms up." Harry lifted his own drink to his lips, one he had been nursing since his bath, and took a long sip. He placed his glass on the tablecloth. "But yes, in answer to your question, it was that bad. The place should be burned to the ground, and its patients set free. You know Spool was part of an Oxford contingent that was conducting quite a disturbing art programme there."

"Disturbing how?"

Lillie had taken her seat beside Harry and she piped up,

"Body parts. They were using them to understand the anatomy of the human body for their art. Apparently it was something Da Vinci used to do and they thought in their infinite wisdom that it would be something the insane might benefit from." She too had been poured a large drink and she took a sip, wincing. "I despise gin," she complained, pushing it away.

"Did you see any of their art?" Petters asked.

"Some, yes. The administrator had a room where some of the paintings were displayed."

"They can't use them in the hallways for fear of the inmates eating them—or was it stealing them? Something like that," Harry expanded, seeing his audience's disapproval.

"So paint, then?" Petters asked. "I mean, it wasn't charcoal or pencil. They were paintings?"

"Yes," Lillie confirmed. "Paint."

"Watercolour or oil?"

"Oil, I believe...yes, certainly oil. Why, what's going on, Felix?"

"I had a sample that I'd taken from the floor of the barn where they were holding Jeremy Winston. Turns out it was oil paint, I've just received the results."

"How is Jeremy, have you seen him today?" Lillie asked.

Harry knew the hospital staff had been very limited with Winston's visitor list. Police and immediate family only, and only during a small window of the day. Lillie had barely squeaked in the previous day.

"I did earlier, yes. He still doesn't remember anything recent. His long-term memory is getting less hazy, though, so there is some hope there."

"Can you really not get me in to see him, Felix? If he can remember anything about past stories, or the lack of them, it might save me quite a lot of time."

"I'll try for tomorrow but don't hold your breath."

Harry clinked the ice in his empty glass and held it up for

Rumple to see. "Back to the paint, you think the paint on the stable floor has something to do with the art programme at Hanwell?"

"Possibly." Petters nodded.

"Or it could have been paint from anything, really. Perhaps someone was using the building to refinish furniture, or was fixing up a car, or a tractor—although why would anyone take the time to repaint a tractor?" Harry watched as Primrose place Lola into her pram and set about for a turn around the garden. "Can you get anything more specific on it?"

"Not much, no. But on the body parts," Petters said to them. "Was there any indication Spool's group were involved in the actual amputation."

"I didn't ask." Lillie gave a shudder. "I suppose I should have."

"Presumably the morgue in Richmond sends the bodies to Hanwell after the post mortem examinations, should they even have them."

"Really, superintendent." Harry felt himself grow nauseous. "Should we pick up this line of discussion *after* dinner? At this rate I won't get through my salad."

They both ignored him and Lillie continued the thread. "If these bodies were intact, presumably someone at Hanwell would have undertaken to preserve them in pieces. Which would have meant some sort of deconstruction."

"Are you suggesting an Oxford *art* student might have done this?" Petters face showed complete disbelief.

"It seems unlikely, doesn't it?" Lillie twirled a piece of hair around her finger. "A medical student, possibly, but hardly an art student."

"There was once an author who went by the name of Octavius Renault," Harry waded in. "A literary genius really, and he would discuss the most grotesque murders in minute detail within his books. It was as though he knew exactly how to carve out a heart or remove one's kidney. Come to think of it now, Renault must have been his pen name." Rumple delivered Harry's gin and tonic and Harry looked up at his manservant with disgust. "You can't be serious, Rumple. What does a man have to do to get a whiskey around here." He sighed, drinking it anyway. "You don't seriously think David Spool had anything to do with this, do you?" Harry questioned.

"I've had some witnesses from the pub murder, although they are all over the place," Petters stated.

"But?" Lillie prompted.

"Well, one nearly blind old lady said she saw a tall woman leaving the pub around the time of the crime." Petters raised his eyebrows. "Of course, around the same time a bricklayer saw a man, also leaving the pub. Or what he thought were the shoes of a man, anyway."

"Presumably the poor chap has his head down all day long. Grim profession," Harry agreed.

"So we aren't really any further along," Lillie concluded.

"No." Petters exhaled as a footman placed a small water-cress salad before him.

"I'll get Primrose," Harry interrupted. "And for goodness sake, where is Jeremiah?"

Lillie received her salad and placed her napkin in her lap. "We'll just have to go back then."

Harry froze at the words. "You must be joking. I can't Lillie, it isn't possible."

"I'll come this time," Petters said, to Harry's great relief. Although he hated to be irrelevant, the whole place gave him the shivers and attempting to return to it would surely set him over the edge.

Primrose took her seat at the table beside him while Rumple took over the pram and continued the turn about the garden. "Come where?" she asked, picking up her fork.

"Hanwell," Lillie answered, giving Harry a teasing glance.

"Oh yes, Harry did fill me in. I remember reading some time ago about the London School of Medicine using the asylum's patients for some research they were doing on muscles and their ability to generate heat. Something about oxygenation and lactic acid, I can't remember specifically, but it does seem as though Hanwell is a veritable hotbed of experimentation, doesn't it?"

Harry shuddered his displeasure at the conversation. "Oh look, there's the main course already."

"Hm." Lillie leaned back so a footman could remove her salad plate.

Harry studied the man and realized he had no earthly idea who he was. Had Rumple been hiring and sacking people on his own accord again? A beautifully plated Dover sole with English pea risotto was placed before each of them. There still wasn't any sign of the elusive Jeremiah.

"Uh, excuse me, have you had the occasion to witness a teenage boy, about yay high, somewhere in the bowels of Rose's kitchen?" Harry asked the new footman.

"Yes sir, he's been at the table for the better part of an hour. She's tasked him with the dessert menu and it does appear to be quite involved."

"Ah, I see. I see. Well, would you be so kind as to ensure the poor boy is fed."

"Yes, sir."

"Prim," Lillie asked. "When was that article you read?"

"Oh goodness, perhaps some time last year. I can't really remember now. It was in one of the London papers."

Lillie raised her eyebrows at Petters. "Do you think it's possible we've missed something?"

"Meaning?"

"Meaning we need to pull a far greater list of people than those just involved in the Oxford programme. We should be looking at the London School of Medicine as well."

"And cross referencing with anyone from Oxford," Petters agreed, seeing where she was going.

"Exactly. Anyone with a medical background." Lillie picked up her fork and pushed the risotto around her plate in thought. "And Felix, I think we should be seriously looking at which patients were involved in both of these programmes. Both the art students and the ones used for the medical testing."

Petters took a large bite of sole and chewed carefully. Swallowing, he said, "Back to Hanwell, Lillie, and soon."

30

The Oxford police station had an eerie quiet about it that evening, like a passenger ship in the last moments before a storm hits—a ghostly wall of white on the horizon moving steadily closer while panicked porters remove the deckchairs and usher guests inside.

There wasn't anyone at the reception desk, which was just as they had planned. It was seven o'clock, dinner time, and the police were nothing if not regimented in their schedules. There would be one or two officers milling about but they had made contingency plans for that.

"It's quite ominous, isn't it?" she said, fading in and out while she pointed one white-flecked finger at the curved receptionist counter.

"Yes, there is no accounting for taste." They both stared at it for a moment, then took in the tall, glassed prisoner box next to it. "Rather like a freak show at the county fair, isn't it." They imagined themselves inside it and then shoved away the thought. "Shall I, then?"

The buzzer was located to the left of the ebony swirled counter and had a brass sign above it that read, *Ring if atten-*

dant is unavailable. She nodded her encouragement and clapped her hands, just as she had in the dress shop. One couldn't help but notice that her attitude had certainly improved. It was a numbers game really, and the more they had under their belts, the happier she became. The pub owner had marked a departure for them. They were doing this, the pieces were falling into place, each one of them a step closer to justice. It wasn't as though they were misguided. No, quite the contrary. They had a very specific battle plan and while there were skirmishes along the way, eventually the war would be won.

The buzzer sounded through the empty hallways of the station, reverberating off the austere stone floor and tossing the sound back at them.

They waited.

Eventually, a middle-aged officer lumbered around the corner to greet them. He huffed his way to the reception counter and settled his bulk on the empty chair.

"What can I help you with?" he sighed audibly, much to their irritation.

He had a bit of his dinner on the side of his mouth and when his lips moved it jiggled. They watched in fascination and thought about betting on when it would fall.

Next sentence, she said. *Second word in.*

"We've come to report a break in," they said, nearly in unison.

"Alright, location please?"

The piece of food dropped to the counter and she held up her hands in victory. The man pulled a pad of paper over and retrieved a pencil from a small jar.

"Just here, outside the station."

The officer looked up, confused.

They elaborated. "It was our car, you see. Someone seems to have sliced the top and stolen quite a few of our belongings."

They hesitated, just for a moment. "I don't suppose Officer Hicks is on shift tonight, is he?"

"You know Hicks?" Instantly his persona changed, they were part of the 'in' crowd.

"Oh yes, he's an old friend of the family."

More like the bastard who did nothing.

"Well, he's here alright but he's on the line at the moment." The hefty officer glanced at the switchboard as though to confirm it.

"We don't mind waiting. It's been such a long time and my mother would be furious with me if I left now and didn't say hello to him."

"Yes, sure thing. Have a seat and I'll send him out when he's off. Oh, and incidentally, your name by the way?"

"Ball," they lied, plucking it out of the air around them then wondering if it would cause Officer Hicks suspicion—someone with a name he didn't recognize alleging they were an old family friend—but they supposed he'd come out of curiosity if nothing else.

The two of them took a seat on a row of scallop-backed chairs and waited.

"He won't recognize you," she said under her breath once the officer had left the reception desk, not that he could hear her anyway.

"Good. I'll make something up about his mother."

"For all you know he's an orphan," she reprimanded. "This is hardly prepared."

"I'm improvising as we go. Stop worrying." Bickering would get them nowhere. They were already there, sitting in the police station while Hicks was no doubt looking for them that very moment—scouring clues and reviewing witness statements about the two dead boys from Oxford and now the pub owner. What kind of fools would walk right in and hand themselves up on a platter? "It isn't as though we have much of a choice. If we want him, we have to come here to get him."

She remained quiet, her legs folded underneath her, arms crossed, the only sound the ticking of a clock from behind the reception desk and the occasional burst of voices from somewhere in the back. It was a sparse room and they should have liked at least a newspaper to read to distract them but they supposed they wouldn't have been able to focus on it anyway.

It took nearly twenty minutes for Hicks to emerge and when he did they wondered if they had the right man. He'd aged in the past few years and they'd hardly got much of a look at him that night anyway in all the commotion. One thing they didn't like was mistakes so they needed to be absolutely sure. There was enough injustice in the world, they should hate to be part of it.

"Officer Hicks?" Although why they were asking was hardly relevant, he was wearing a name badge on his uniform.

"You've got him." Hicks studied them. Well, the one he could see anyway. "How can I help?" He had a fleshy face that spoke of poor genes and too much food. His nose was broad and flat, his eyes hooded. They pegged him at fifty, or nearly so.

"You probably don't remember me, my mother and yours used to be acquaintances." Admittedly it would have been an odd union, in all likelihood the two woman would have been almost a generation apart.

"No, I'm sorry, I don't."

At least he had a mother and they were on somewhat solid ground.

"Of course not, it was some time ago now." Should they elaborate? Probably not since they'd made it all up to this point and didn't really need to except for the purposes of conversation. "We...I'd just thought I'd ask for you anyway. You see, I have had a little mishap with my car and thought to myself, well, why not see if I can't go and find Officer Hicks to help me out."

"I see." Hicks was looking at them strangely, as though he were trying to place them but couldn't.

He can't remember, she said with frustration, defeat written all over her face, or the pieces of it that could be seen anyway.

"Yes," they continued. "It's just outside here, I wonder if you could come and have a look. It appears to have been vandalized."

"Anything stolen?"

"Oh, you know, a few things. The scoundrel has absconded with a particularly rare silver trinket box. Georgian, with an enamel face."

Hicks was scribbling something down as they talked.

"They've also taken a Scottish sterling breakfast set and it's matching tea caddy. I'm a bit of a collector, you see, so I do tend to have these things here and there and I happened to have a few pieces with me today. It doesn't sound like much, granted, but all together it adds up to a tidy sum."

"I see." Hicks finished writing and placed the pad of paper on the desk. "I suppose I better come out and have a look."

That'll be a first, she said with contempt, scowling at him.

Hicks came out from behind the reception desk and followed them outside to the car, which they had conveniently parked a little way down the road and to the left of a dishevelled church graveyard, its dark body huddled discreetly under a bunch of overgrown oaks, their branches reaching down nearly to the pavement and plucking at their hair as they studied the car. They had sliced the roof themselves and it gaped like a flesh wound.

"I see they've done quite a job of it, haven't they." Hicks peered up over the roof into the car.

They opened one of the rear doors and stood back. "If you

have a look here you can see where the silver was kept. Perhaps they've left some trace of themselves?"

"If they did, it won't likely be enough to go on but I'll have a look, certainly." Hicks ducked his head and moved his body across the back seat.

"It was just there on the floor." They pointed.

"Yes." Hicks bent at the hips and studied the floor of the car where the imaginary silver must have been kept.

Now, she urged. *Now*.

They wouldn't have much time and they watched the policeman's uniformed back as they pulled the knife from a pocket, the very same knife they had slashed the roof of the car with. He was muttering something about the breakdown of law and order in Oxford and the difficulty in tracing thieves as they plunged the knife into that uniformed back, watching the blood seep into the fabric, darkening it while he squirmed and gasped, clutching the seat in front of him as though it would save him from imminent death.

Once more for good measure, she commanded.

How could one disobey a dead girl?

The second stab wound finished him and he slumped forward at an unnatural angle, his head pressed into the back of the front seat.

At least he's in the correct place for a drive through town, she maintained, *I should hate to have to give up my seat to that swine.*

"Mm. Yes. We will wait for darkness to fall and then drop him off."

With a flash of coral and a warranted determination, they slammed the back door of the car and sped off into the Oxford twilight.

31

DANIEL

He had chosen a location that wasn't far from the train station. A much-frequented pub at the intersection where the road curved, it provided an excellent viewpoint from where he could watch the steady stream of travellers leaving the station, crossing the canal and emerging into the subdued twilight of a university city on summer break. Most students had headed home for a few months, to locales across England and abroad, and those that remained for the odd summer tutorial had adopted the relaxed composure of the advantaged—tanned skin and impeccably tousled hair cuts, Egyptian cotton dress shirts, cuffs rolled to their elbows. Daniel despised them on sight.

He had chosen a small table by the window and knew his targets would be travelling as a pair. It wouldn't be difficult to pick out a couple of Americans in a crowd of English. It was the little things. The curve of their fedora, the make of their shoes, their arrogant body language—the set of the shoulders and the tilt of their heads. They hardly knew it themselves. They would be on the seven twenty from London; he glanced at the Rolex on his wrist. It should have already arrived so he wouldn't be waiting long.

His source had been exceedingly forthcoming, although perhaps it was the knife at his throat that made him so. Daniel had drawn a thin ribbon of blood to ensure the man knew he had meant business. That and he had threatened his wife— something he didn't usually like to do, but it couldn't be helped this time. Daniel knew what the men were coming for. It wasn't anything surprising—it was what they always came for. Or one of two things anyway. Money was one. Revenge was the other. This time, it was the latter.

He waited.

A waitress moved quickly through the room, tray in hand, and stopped at his table. "Can I get you anything?"

Daniel held up his empty glass. "Another, please."

She nodded and hurried off in the direction of the bar, her head full of orders.

He had been there for half an hour and noticed that he had become nervous while he waited. Something new for him. Was it because he was about to have a confrontation in Lillie's home town? And now there wasn't just her to worry about but the baby as well?

He glanced again at his watch. Seven forty-five. Shouldn't they have been here by now? He eyed the road across the canal. An elderly couple struggled with their bags, a woman and her school-aged boy hurried in front of them, a lone man obviously from the city and enjoying the slower pace of Oxford sauntered along slowly, stopping on the bridge to admire the view.

No sign of the two men from New York.

Frustrated, Daniel thought about leaving. Had he been fed a bunch of lies?

The waitress dropped a fresh beer on the table and Daniel reached into his pocket to pay his bill as she did so. He didn't really want his drink now, fighting back the trepidation in his stomach. Could they have circumvented him somehow? But why? Didn't they want to find him? Unless...the thought sent shivers down his spine. What better way to get back at him than to find something dear to him and destroy it. He stood up, nearly knocking over his drink in the process. Did they know about Lillie? Was *she* actually their target? He snatched up his light overcoat and headed towards the door.

32

LILLIE

L illie pushed Lola's pram up Cornmarket Street and turned left onto the main thoroughfare of Broad Street.

It had been a particularly appealing day and the twilight had quickly crept orange and violet across an electric blue sky, now promising a handsome reveal of stars. They'd been later than Lillie had expected, leaving Harry's and stopping in at the newspaper to see if there had been anything new from their search of Jeremy's office before heading home. Still nothing. Lola would be expecting her bottle shortly. Nanny had headed to London for the day to visit her daughter. As Lola began to fuss, Lillie stopped to adjust her blanket, leaning over her baby and making faces only a mother would dare make in public. Lola gurgled what Lillie hoped was amusement and she began to push the pram a little more quickly, the last thing she needed was for Lola to have a full scale meltdown in the middle of Oxford. Jiggling the pram as she walked was the only weapon she had to ward off certain evening disaster—it was the witching hour, after all.

They weren't far from home and as she left the bustle of the summer Oxford evening behind, she found, as she often did, that she enjoyed the solace of her thinly populated neighbourhood. She reached her cottage and opened the iron gate, hearing the comforting squeak of its hinges. Had it been Felix Petters' gate, it would have been oiled ages ago but Lillie liked it when things began to feel lived in. Her now deceased parents had built their Manhattan brownstone when she was five and Lillie still remembered how her mother had been thrilled when the wood floor in the kitchen had finally developed a squeak in one of the boards. It was the demarcation between new and lived-in, she'd explained to Lillie one morning as they had made breakfast together. It was what made a home a home. Lillie hadn't understood it at all at the time, but she did now.

It was nearly nine o'clock, she noted, listening to the steady tick of the enormous grandfather clock in her front entrance. She lifted Lola out of the pram and headed to the kitchen to warm her bottle, thinking she would skip her bath tonight. On the salt-scrubbed table Lola's bassinet, a gift from Harry and Primrose, sat waiting and Lillie placed the baby inside while she went to the sink. As she warmed the bottle she was serenaded by coos from the table, a flutter of tiny fists and feet barely visible above the sides of the woven basket.

The dark had begun to creep across the sky but Lillie saw a flutter of something outside the kitchen window that caught her attention. It was fleeting, and because she was in a bit of a trance when it happened, she wondered if she'd even imagined it—although the disconnect between the empty back yard and something crossing in front of her window put her on instant alert. A wayward sheep? A Shetland pony who'd escaped its herd? It was too early for Daniel and he wouldn't have been creeping around the back garden anyway. He came directly to the kitchen door and let himself in with the key she'd had cut for him.

Lillie carefully placed the bottle in a warm bowl of water in the sink and opened the kitchen door. She stared out into the yard, hopeful she would catch whatever domestic creature had gone rogue but instead felt, rather than saw, a hand grab her forearm and push her firmly and abruptly back into the kitchen. Startled, she tripped over the threshold and lost her balance, only to be swiftly righted by the same hand that had caught her off guard in the first place.

"Stay inside!" Daniel hissed, stepping into the house after her and slamming the door shut behind him.

"What the..." She was cut short by the look of sheer anger on his face, as though it had been etched on his jawline by a knife.

"How long have you been here?" he demanded, voice lowered.

"I just walked in the door. Why? What's going on?"

Daniel picked up the bassinet from the table and cradled it in his arms. "Follow me," he said, glancing out the kitchen window into the night. "Right now, Lillie," he commanded, seeing her hesitate.

Feeling her chest tighten, she grabbed the bottle out of the sink and hurried behind him into the entry hallway and up the stairs to the bedroom. Whatever was going on was serious enough to have Daniel take the chance of showing up to her house early. When they reached the bedroom he placed the bassinet on the bed and drew the curtains closed. Lillie went to the bedside and turned on a lamp.

"Tell me." She spoke softly, not knowing if he was worried about someone inside the house with them or not.

"I don't know if they've beat me here or not," he mumbled, running one hand through his short hair.

"Who?"

He didn't answer and instead of pushing him Lillie gathered up Lola and began to feed her the prepared bottle. Whatever was going on wouldn't be helped by a crying baby. As far as she could tell, the house was just as quiet as it had been when she'd arrived home so whoever Daniel thought was coming hadn't materialized yet.

"Don't leave this room," he warned her, as he headed back towards the door. "Doesn't it lock?" He stared at the door knob plate.

"No."

"Don't leave," he reiterated, frowning at her as though to make his point, which was hardly necessary. Lillie could see as plain as day that whatever trouble had followed Daniel back from America was now here on her doorstep.

Lillie finished feeding Lola and watched as her precious baby fell asleep in her arms. Carefully, she lifted her back into the bassinet and covered her with a light blanket. Then she perched on the edge of the bed and waited, straining her ears against the silence of the night air.

Nothing.

Not a sound to tell her anything was wrong at all.

At least fifteen minutes passed before she heard a creak on the stairs and she fought against her better judgement to go onto the landing and have a look at who was coming. It had to be Daniel. Surely he was overreacting, was he not? No one was in the house.

The door knob to her bedroom turned and Lillie positioned herself in front of the bassinet, feeling a deep anger rise inside her as surely as the fear it pushed away. If anyone thought for one minute they were going to harm her baby they could think again.

Lillie tensed. What was this all about? Had Daniel's past caught up with him? Was this why he had gone back to America while she had stayed on in Provence without him?

The door nudged open, carefully, hesitantly, just the slightest bit.

Lillie got up from the bed, wishing she had something with

her she could clobber the intruder over the head with. Her heart beat with the cadence of a hummingbird's wings and a chill ran down her back.

A dark head came around the corner of the door and Lillie drew in her breath, poised and ready.

"Lillie?" Felix Petters pushed open the door a little further and stepped into her bedroom.

"Felix!" Lillie exhaled, realizing she'd been holding her breath. "What are you doing here?"

"I got a call saying there was an intruder in your house." He glanced quickly around the room then looked back out into the hallway.

"I never called," Lillie blurted it out and then regretted it immediately. Daniel must have thought he needed help. Whatever was going on was enough to scare him into using traditional law enforcement. That made her even more frightened.

"No, it was a man, but from this number. Who've you got here?"

Lillie sat silently. She wasn't going to lie to him but nor would she throw Daniel under the lorry's tyres.

Seeing he wasn't getting anywhere with her he gave up the line of questioning. "I've secured the inside of the house, but there's no way of knowing who is lingering outside. You and Lola will come with me tonight. Have you anything you need to take with you?"

Lillie nodded and began gathering a few personal items which she then stuffed into a bag she retrieved from her wardrobe. She zipped across the hall to the nursery and grabbed a few napkins and some extra clothes for Lola. When she was ready, she flung the bag over her shoulder and gathered up a sleeping Lola, carefully wrapping her in a wool baby blanket and following Petters into the darkened hallway and down the stairs.

"I need some bottles," she said, putting down her bag on

the floor by the front door and heading through into the kitchen. She wondered where Daniel had gone, was he outside watching the house? With Petters' arrival had he decided it was safe to leave?

She entered the pantry and reached up to retrieve a couple of bottles, as she did so she heard a soft click behind her. She turned to call for Felix but before she could she found herself staring into the barrel of a small pistol. Lillie clutched Lola to her chest and instinctively turned her body to protect her sleeping baby.

"Please..." she whispered, feeling the words catch in her throat.

"Where is he?" The man holding the gun looked about as terrifying as a man could. He wasn't overly tall, or overly large, but he wore a face that told of years on the flip side of gentrified society. He had a large scar over his left eye and one cheek was sunken, as though the bone had once been mashed to a pulp and left in pieces with his skin acting like its very own teabag.

"I honestly don't know, but he isn't here with us. Please, she's a baby, for God's sake." Lillie refused to turn and face the man head on, sheltering Lola from him.

"Lillie," came Petters' strained voice from the foyer. There must have been two of them otherwise Petters would have been in there with her. Had he been restrained? "Lillie, listen to me very carefully. Give the man what he's asking for. There isn't any point sheltering anyone. It's your life, Lillie, and Lola's."

Lillie didn't think for one minute that the man holding a gun to them would be letting them go after she gave up Daniel. More likely he would shoot them all and then do the same to Daniel. But none of that changed things. Daniel had been there minutes before and now he had vanished.

"I don't know where he is. I'm telling you the honest—" She was cut off abruptly by a hand reaching around the man's body and with one swift swipe of an arm the gun was knocked away from his hands. It clattered to the flagstone floor and skidded across it. Lillie stood stone still, mouth gaping as Daniel threw his body between the man and her and Lola, simultaneously reaching back to push them behind him with one arm while he kicked the man hard in the chest and sent him spinning to the floor. Daniel stepped forward and in one smooth movement retrieved the gun from the flagstones, raised his hands and levelled it directly at the man's chest. Taking one fearful look at him, the man began to scramble backwards, half crawling, half walking in a desperate but futile attempt to get away.

"Daniel!" Lillie shouted at him, causing Lola to startle and wail. What she wanted was for him to stop before he made a decision he couldn't change. Felix was there, they were now at least half in control of the situation and he could arrest the men, take them to the station and hold them until they could ascertain who they were and what they were doing there. "Daniel, please," she tried again, pleading with him. He turned to look at her and she sensed he was almost confused in his focus, but she immediately saw the anger in his eyes and knew. She had little to no right to judge him for it—these men had come into his world, into her home, and threatened them all.

The sound of the gunshot echoed off the plate-glass windows of her little cottage and dissipated with the sounds of whimpering. It took Lillie a minute to realize it was her own. Daniel, seeing her there, tears rolling down her cheeks, holding a crying baby clutched to her chest let his face crumple—a map of splattered blood from the man who now lay certainly dead on the floor beneath him.

At this point and unbeknownst to them, another struggle between Petters and the dead man's accomplice had ensued in the foyer which resulted in yet another gunshot going off, the bullet obviously hitting a window in the living room as the shatter of glass echoed into the kitchen. Lola's wailing increased to a crescendo while simultaneously Petters entered the kitchen shoving the man in front of him, gun cocked, blood oozing down the policeman's cheek. He took one look at the dead man on the floor then raised his eyes to Daniel's. He looked at Lillie, long and hard, then sat the man down on one of her kitchen chairs and used a set of handcuffs to keep him there.

"I'll need the telephone," he said as matter-of-factly as if he were asking for a cup of coffee and Lillie motioned towards the alcove off the kitchen, finding her words were failing her. "You want to tell me what's going on?" He looked to Daniel who engaged his stare but silently shook his head, stepping back from the mess on the floor. Was this it? Was it all over for them? Petters would arrest him now—even though *this* Daniel could explain it away as self-defence. The important point was that Petters now knew Lillie was still in touch with an assassin who had killed two members of a wartime committee. Daniel was a wanted man and was standing right in front of the officer who had once tracked him until Daniel had fled back to New York.

She jiggled Lola in her arms and the baby began to quieten down which was more than could be said for the pit in Lillie's stomach. She looked at the dead man on the floor in front of her and fought the urge to vomit.

"You brought them here, *right to her*. You realize that, don't you?" Petters accused.

Daniel nodded but remained silent.

"Her and her baby were nearly killed here tonight."

"Yes, sir," Daniel answered, deferentially. Something he definitely wasn't.

"Yes, well. Will this be the last of them?"

"I certainly hope so." Daniel didn't look so sure.

"She obviously loves you." Petters sighed, looking at Lillie and Lola with a slow dawning of recognition. He stared at the baby, then back at Daniel. "Sweet Jesus, Lillie—you've got to be joking. Is she...?"

Lillie was mute. Everything that had transpired in her little cottage that night had shaken her ideal Oxford life and she felt her eyes well with tears, it was about to come to a grinding halt. Daniel took a step towards her as though he wanted to comfort her.

"Stop right there." Petters aimed the gun he was still holding at Daniel's head.

"Shoot me if you have to," Daniel responded. "But I'm not ever leaving this woman."

He bridged the distance between them with two long strides but Lillie involuntarily backed away from him, causing him to pause. She knew he'd been an assassin, of course she did, but seeing him actually *kill a man*, this was different somehow—there was a monumental divide between knowing something and seeing it unfold. He searched her eyes but she let them drop to the floor so he wouldn't see the horror. He waited, giving her a minute to gather her thoughts, and then took the final step towards her, gathering both of them into his arms.

33

SUPERINTENDENT FELIX PETTERS

"What do you mean Hicks is missing? Since bloody when?"

Superintendent Felix Petters slumped back in his office chair, dabbing at the wound on his face, and glanced up at the clock on the station wall while he ran his hand through his bristled hair. It was just after midnight and it'd been a hell of a night. He thought of Lola's baby blanket marked with blood, Lillie embracing a man who'd been on his wanted list for years, and him, the Oxford Police Superintendent allowing a criminal to walk right out of his hands as easily as the man had walked right out of Lillie's front door. He'd been helpless to stop him. Petters had taken in the entire scene—the past, the future, the love he saw in Lillie's eyes and in turn that very same adoration reflected back in his—how could he possibly break up that bond? It had been the first time in his life that he'd had to make a decision that completely contradicted the oath he had taken as a police officer.

"Around seven thirty this evening." His overnight officer answered, bringing Petters' thoughts back to the present. He could analyze his breakdown in ethics later.

"Missing as in he went for his supper and never came back?"

"Originally that was what I thought, he went out to check on a vehicle break-in but didn't return. I figured he'd just decided to grab a bite while he was out there and since he was off at nine, perhaps he just called it a night."

"And...?" Petters was annoyed with the speed of the conversation.

"Well, sir—I just realized he left his lunch kit here. He'd packed himself a dinner and it's untouched. He also left his house keys here so it's unlikely he's gone home."

"It's been over four hours!" Petters sputtered. "You've got an officer missing for four hours and you only thought to follow up on that now? Have you sent anyone around to his house to see if he is there?"

"Just now, yes. Higgins went. He's not there. His wife says she hasn't seen him or heard from him since he left at noon."

"Right." Felix hauled himself out of his chair and headed towards a large open area of the station where he routinely gathered officers and support staff for emergency situations. Which is exactly what they had now. "Round them up," he barked to the overnight officer. "I'll get Rosemary to summon the on-calls."

His late night receptionist wasn't supposed to be there past midnight but she hadn't yet left and on hearing his voice immediately put her head down and began to work the switchboard. Within five minutes Felix had the entire skeleton force gathered around him. There were only six of them but it was enough to get started. The on-calls would begin filing in shortly but he could come up with a search plan in the meantime.

"Who took the original inquiry about car break-in, was it Hicks?"

Higgins put up his hand. "I did, superintendent."

"Telephone or in person?" Felix asked.

"In person, sir."

"Male or female?"

"Female."

"Description?" Felix looked around at his men and frowned at a couple of them who were murmuring to each other. "Everyone listen up!"

"Youngish, tall, straight, shoulder-length hair, sort of mousy in colour."

"Be more specific." Felix was irritated. "Brown, blonde?"

"Brown. Definitely brown."

"Good. Build?"

"I'm sorry, sir?"

"Her build, Higgins. Heavy, thin, moderate?"

"She seemed..." the officer paused. "Strong. Not heavy or thin but well-muscled. As though she did farm work perhaps."

"Yes, that's good. Someone who possibly did manual labour. And how young was she, would you say? Twenties? Thirties?"

"I wasn't with her long so I didn't really get much of a look but I'd say late twenties. She said Hicks was a family friend or something. I'm trying to remember exactly."

"So she asked for him by name, then?" That changed things for a start. If this woman was responsible for Hicks's disappearance, she knew him. It wasn't lost on Felix that the description Higgins was giving them sounded ominously like the same description the old lady had given them after the pub murder. A tall woman with hair like a curtain.

A *wig*, Jeremiah had argued. Were they dealing with the same person? A wig would mean that she could be changing her hair as often as she changed her clothing.

"Right." Felix didn't want to waste any time. He dabbed again at his cheek as he felt the flesh wound he had received at Lillie's ooze blood down his face. He'd forgo the incident report, saying he tripped going up the stairs if anyone asked. Not that they had. He'd reluctantly released the dead man's accomplice onto the last train to London with a grave message that if he ever came back to Oxford he'd lock him up for life. Although he half wondered now if Daniel wouldn't hunt him down and neatly dispose of him. The man was absolutely terrifying when he was backed into a corner and no doubt the attack on his beloved wouldn't do much to improve his mood. "Let's break off into groups of two. I want the area around the station combed through very carefully first. Take torches and don't miss an inch of ground. When the on-calls arrive, let's branch out and divide the city into quadrants. We've got an officer missing and presumed in distress."

If Hicks was sitting in a pub somewhere, Petters would skin him alive. He hadn't ever been Felix's favourite officer—there was always a bit of a chip on his shoulder and he tended to drink too much, often leaving work early or arriving late because of it. Last year he'd got into an incident with a man they'd arrested for being disorderly in public. Hicks had dragged him into the station and laid into him a little too aggressively. When Felix had reprimanded him for it Hicks had nearly exploded. It wasn't a huge thing and Felix had brushed it aside as hot-headedness but it was enough that he thought of it now.

"Rosemary!" Felix called to the receptionist. She spun around in her seat, telephone still in hand. "It's going to be a long night, I'm sorry to report."

"It won't be the first, nor that last," she commiserated. "You don't even need to say it superintendent. I'll pull everything Hicks has worked on. How far back?"

Petters liked an employee that anticipated rather than waited for direction. "Three years, and—"

"Coffee," she finished for him, getting up and heading to the kitchen.

34

LILLIE

"You look terrible," Jeremy Winston observed early the next morning as he sat, fully clothed in a fisherman's sweater and dark brown trousers, on the end of his hospital bed. He folded the newspaper he was reading and slapped it down beside him.

Lillie didn't doubt it after the night she'd had. She glanced down at the white blouse and ankle length skirt she wore, half expecting to see blood splatter even though it was a perfectly clean outfit she had pulled from her closet that morning. She hadn't slept of course, spending the night scrubbing her kitchen floor again and again after Daniel had cleaned up the body and removed it to God only knew where. Finally at three in the morning she had slumped against the kitchen wall and had allowed Daniel to gently remove the scrub brush from her blood-stained hands and lift her into the warm bath he'd drawn for her. She'd sat there, numb to the world and listening for Lola's cries, only to be rewarded with a silent house and the wash of water over her skin as Daniel gently bathed her with the same hands that he had just carried out the body with.

When he'd finished he'd taken her to bed and held her while she'd wept quietly into his shoulder. He'd circled her with his arms, kissing away her tears and promising her she was safe. She didn't really know whether she was or not but she knew he would do everything in his power to make sure nothing happened to them. When she'd left early that morning after dropping Lola at Nanny's, grateful the woman had returned on a late train well after the whole incident, she'd seen Daniel and two men walking the perimeter of her property. They looked like ex-army and Lillie wondered if they'd been deployed in Belgium with Daniel in 1917? How else would he get help *that* quickly in a country that was not his own? All in all though, it had given her some solace that at least temporarily they would be safe.

Lillie looked at her boss and wondered if he was getting ready to flee. "Going somewhere, Jeremy?"

"The newspaper."

"You are? Are you sure?" Surely he was being ridiculous and petulant. He wasn't ready to go anywhere yet.

"I'm exhibiting the picture of perfect health so these ninnies can let me out of here. It's not like I can't remember if I left the stove on or not—I'm not having that much trouble with my memory, for goodness sakes. Sitting in a hospital being constantly interrupted by doctors and nurses is hardly conducive to recovery." He motioned to the newspaper with a flick of his hand. "And look at this reporting, Lillie. Are you not reviewing each and every article that is being put out?"

She wasn't, of course, not even close. They were far too big a newspaper for her to do that and maintain her job as lead crime reporter. "Don't be silly."

"About the newspaper or about leaving this dreadful place?"

"Both."

Jeremy glared defiantly at her.

"Do you really not remember a thing about your ordeal?" she tried, knowing full well the police had covered everything with him to no avail.

"I honestly don't remember a thing past talking to you the morning you came back to the office after being in France. It's as though time has just been erased." He rubbed at his head as though he could force his memory back through brute willpower.

Lillie frowned, remembering their conversation. "You seemed jumpy that morning."

"I did?"

If Jeremy knew what she was talking about he wasn't letting on. He seemed completely confused at the suggestion.

"Perhaps I was just busy?" he asked her. "I can't remember much about my mindset at the time."

"Possibly. Anyway, I'll bring you up to speed. We've been trying to find anything in your files that might have to do with someone wanting to kidnap you. Since you seem to have your long-term memory, any chance you might be able to point us in the right direction?"

"Stories I've covered that were controversial?"

"Possibly. Anything that might have to do with the two Oxford rowers?"

"Not that I know of. And isn't being controversial just par for the course? We are reporters, for Christ's sake." Jeremy looked as though he were annoyed at the whole thing. "What do we cover that *isn't* controversial?"

"Politics maybe? Social unrest? It has to be something local. Every death to this point has been of a local Oxford citizen. Originally I thought because our first and second victims both came from York there might have been something in that, perhaps the dead girl in the river, but I can't seem to find anything that sticks."

Jeremy nodded. "I've just heard about the pub victim."

"Not an Oxford student."

"No."

Lillie looked at her friend. He'd lost a significant amount of weight in the short time he'd been away from them. His hand was bandaged where his finger had been removed and she gave a shudder at what he must have had to go through. It was no wonder his subconscious had chosen to forget. "And then you. They let *you* go, but not the others. Why?"

Jeremy gave her a hard stare to suggest he didn't really want to have to repeat himself.

"Yes, yes. I know. It'll come," she assured him, referring to his memory.

"I certainly hope so because living like this is infuriating."

"I can imagine," Lillie commiserated.

The door to the hospital room opened and a sprightly nurse poked her head in. Jeremy instantly perked up at the sight of her. "Doctor will be in shortly, Mr Winston. Although you'll have a tough job of convincing him."

When she was gone Lillie added, "I agree."

"Oh hush." Jeremy waved her away.

"Why do you think they took your finger?" Lillie motioned to his bandaged hand and Jeremy glanced down at it, giving the bandage a rub with his other hand.

"I really don't know," he answered.

"And Edwin Hastock's head, Andrew Baker's arm, the pub owner's ear..."

"All of us with missing body parts." Jeremy nodded. "It's grisly, no doubt about that. I got off easy, all things considered." He rubbed at his chin. "Lillie...what if it was something we didn't cover but should have?"

"I've thought of that, yes."

"It would have to be something very personal for someone to act like this in retaliation."

"I agree." Lillie nodded. "And I strongly believe it would have had to have involved murder, or at the very least an accidental death."

"In Oxford, most likely," Jeremy continued. "Or the immediate surrounding area."

He got up as though he would follow her from the hospital room that instant to get straight to work.

"Sit," Lillie commanded. "I'll start with the police files, assuming Petters will give me access."

Jeremy nodded. "Anyone dead or missing over the last five years."

"Cross referenced with our past story log."

"If we didn't report on it, chances are someone is extremely angry."

"Got it, boss, I'll get going right away." Lillie stood up and slung her brown leather bag over her shoulder, ready to get to work.

SHE LEFT Jeremy's room and headed west down the hospital corridor to the bank of stairs at the far end of the floor which she then took two at a time, emerging into a nearly full hospital waiting room. There was a heavy police presence clustered to one end around a stationary gurney and she stopped in surprise to observe it. Whoever was on the stretcher was covered head to toe in a long ivory sheet. For a moment Lillie felt a panicky surge that something had happened to Felix and she raced over to the group to find out what was going on.

Before she could reach them a voice called out to her. "Lillie!" She spun around to see a harried Felix Petters rushing towards her.

"Thank goodness, Felix!" she exclaimed to him. "I had a horrible thought something had just happened to you. After last night and everything—."

Felix cut her off. "Something has happened. We've had an officer killed, last night."

"Oh no, you haven't." Lillie glanced morbidly towards the covered gurney. "Who?"

"Officer Hicks. Stabbed to death." Felix winced the words.

"Where was he?"

"He'd gone to check on a vehicle break-in near the station but his body was found on the north side of town."

"The killer moved him?"

"Yes, it would seem so." He looked pensive.

Lillie had known her friend long enough to know he wasn't giving her the whole of it. She waited, searching his face for more. "And?" she finally prompted.

"Lillie—whoever it was removed his eyes. Actually carved them out."

Lillie fought back the urge to vomit at the visual imagery of that. She nodded her understanding. "What was he working on?"

"Nothing of importance. Certainly nothing that would warrant this kind of action."

"Related to the others, then?"

"It would certainly seem so, wouldn't it?"

"Could be." She agreed. "We need to get back to Hanwell."

"I can't possibly go now, Lillie, I've got a full-scale man hunt going on here. And speaking of"—he lowered his voice—"what exactly are you doing about the incident last night?"

"It's taken care of, Felix." She thought about thanking him for not arresting Daniel on the spot but decided the less said about the matter the better. At least for now. They had enough to concentrate on with a serial killer wandering around Oxford, they didn't need to deal with Daniel's history as well—there wasn't much they could do about it anyway.

"What can I write about this?" She changed the subject.

"Not much yet, I'll let you know but follow up on Hanwell

as soon as you can." Felix spun on his heel, effectively ending their conversation, and walked towards his huddle of officers.

35

The front door of the *Oxford Daily Press* had been propped open rather unceremoniously with yesterday's hastily folded newspaper. Someone had shoved it awkwardly underneath the gap between the door and the top of the shallow and worn stone steps leading up to it.

You can't be serious, she stated in disbelief, while they stood at the street, gazing up at the second-storey windows which had also been opened to let the heat escape. The whir of the printing presses punctuated the lazy calm of a Thursday afternoon on Cornmarket Street.

"Dead serious."

They both laughed at this, as though it were the most hysterical thing they'd ever heard. Neither of them had had enough sleep and their fatigue was making them giddy.

It's not really a good idea.

"I'm not asking you to walk into a police station."

We've already done that. She gave a hard stare that illustrated the gravity of what they had just done. *I really don't see what we hope to achieve from this, other than possibly getting caught and thrown into that horrible glass case at said police station.* She frowned her disagreement and flicked her hair back. The light caught it, reflecting bits of blonde amongst the cinnamon. Was it getting lighter with the sun? It always had. There was one summer in particular when the temperatures had soared and the two of them had spent hours by the river, lazily discussing the state of the post-war world, debating the merits of cubism and surrealism and whether or not Bauhaus was an acceptable choice for the emerging skyscrapers of New York—something neither of them had ever seen.

"I wish we had gone there together." The nostalgia of the memories were overpowering, as though they could still smell the river, feel the long grass pluck at their clothes and itch their ankles. It was as though if they looked up they would see the hawks hunting the field mice and the magic of balloon clouds that appeared to be too perfect to be real.

New York, she echoed. She didn't need to be told, she was always inside their thoughts. One only had to think it with her.

"Well." A deep breath in and then an exhale to release the tension and let the negative thoughts go. Just as had been taught by psychoanalyst after psychoanalyst. "Shall we, then?"

If you insist this is the only way.

"She is the lead crime reporter, shouldn't she be the one to write it?"

All they wanted was for everyone to know exactly what had happened. Was that too much to ask for? Their lives had been ruined—torn from them without so much as a ripple in the collective consciousness. Didn't they deserve some attention? Some retribution?

They stepped up the concave steps and into the muggy-aired reception of the *Oxford Daily Press*.

36

DANIEL

The shaded garden of Orchard Cottage was the ideal refuge for a man at his wits' end. Daniel sat at the far end of it on a rock wall bordering an enormous hay field. He felt the rough edge of a sharp rock, running his fingers back and forth over it as though it might jerk him out of his reverie. Staring back at the main house and the miniature cottage which for the moment housed Lola and her nanny, he was struck with an almost sudden burst of nostalgia. For what? he wondered. He'd certainly never had a bucolic setting such as this one as part of his life. He'd grown up in the dark under-belly of American cities, his cohorts being either criminals or those aspiring to be so. But sitting under this walnut tree, surrounded by wild pink roses and thatched roofs, the occasional whinny of a neighbouring pony and the rustle of a warm summer breeze through the leaves above him—well, it made him want to stay forever. Something he couldn't possibly do now. Not after what had happened last night and would be sure to happen again the longer he stayed. He was putting the love of his life at great personal risk, both her and their baby. Not to mention what she must think of him.

He dropped his head into his hands and ran his fingers agitatedly through his short hair. There just wasn't any way around it. He'd have to head back to New York and put to bed those who were coming for him. Either that or make their lives here a veritable fortress of defence, dealing with each degenerate that came for them, one by one, until there were none left. It wasn't surprising really, after the life he'd led. He'd always known they'd likely come for retribution but until now he'd only had himself to worry about. He'd never had anyone else he'd truly cared for. *Loved*. He had been naive until now. And now there was Lillie. And Lola. And he loved them more than he'd ever thought possible. They were his.

"We've secured the perimeter," said an Irish accented voice behind him. "Sir?"

The man before him had been an exceptional soldier and Daniel knew he would be the help he needed to guard Lillie's place. Back in 1914 Paddy had neatly defended their small British-American contingent from an upper storey window on the abandoned and burning cloth hall tower in Ypres while Daniel had ushered seven of their best sharpshooters out of the city and into the countryside. The Irishman had stayed with them until Passchendaele in seventeen when he was invalided out with a leg wound. He still limped, all these years later, but he hadn't lost any of his exceptional ability with a rifle. Daniel had known exactly where to find him and had sent an emergency telegram to his London office that morning. Now in private security, Paddy had caught the first train to Oxford emerging bright-eyed onto the platform at eight o'clock that morning no questions asked, much to Daniel's relief. He'd brought a small group of three men, and Daniel caught a glimpse of one of them in the distance as they methodically circled the cottage, barely visible to a passerby.

It gave him at least a modicum of confidence.

"Thank you," Daniel said to him.

"You've got them as long as you need them." Paddy nodded. "They'll alternate shifts."

"I'll have the funds sent your office today." Daniel replied.

It wouldn't be cheap but money wasn't really something Daniel needed to worry about. No, what he needed to worry about was getting Lillie protection against the next men who came looking for him. And the ones after that, and the ones after that. What a fool he had been to come after her. They'd said their goodbyes in Provence and he'd had every intention of returning to America without her. It was for her own good, he'd argued to himself again and again, right up to the minute he boarded the ship to Southampton and threw all reason out the window. The thing was, he'd realized very quickly that a life without Lillie wasn't a life worth living. He was lucky Superintendent Petters hadn't arrested him on the spot last night.

He shook Paddy's hand, then continued, "Listen, I'm going to have to leave and head back to America to look after some business." *That was one way of putting it.* "Can you assure me you'll have this place guarded day and night, I don't care what it costs."

"Of course. How long will you be gone?"

"Just long enough to do away with whoever is coming for me."

"I assume you know who it is?" Paddy asked.

Daniel nodded solemnly. "I wouldn't be surprised if that punk Lucky Luciano is wanting to use my demise as his way back in. He was just arrested on heroin peddling to a couple of undercovers. He's gotten off but he's looking for a way back in —what with his reputation in shreds. Doing away with a former member who went rogue should do it nicely."

Paddy knew Daniel's history so he didn't have any trouble giving him the full picture. Paddy's own involvement with the

Irish Republican Army after the war meant he was far from squeaky clean himself. A colonel had once told Daniel in passing that men on the fringe made the best soldiers—perhaps there was some truth to that, as contradictory as it seemed.

Paddy gave him a rueful smile. "Hurry back, my friend."

37

LILLIE

T ynesmore sat nestled and majestic amongst the rolling fields of Oxfordshire. It had been an unusually active summer of monarch butterflies and two of them greeted Lillie, dancing perilously close to the end of her nose as she parked her bicycle and crunched across the gravel to the enormous oak front doors that had been thrown open to the heated afternoon. Constance, Harry's enormous Irish wolfhound, wandered out, giving her a cursory sniff en route to the shade of a heavily adorned walnut tree to the side of the house.

"Hello?" Lillie called, as she entered unannounced into the vast foyer. She was greeted with the smell of lilies and lilacs. Or was it jasmine? She could never be sure which was which and Tynesmore never had any shortage of fresh flowers. "Prim? Harry?"

"Up here," came Harry's voice from his dressing room at the top of the stairs.

Lillie glanced up and then began to ascend the curved staircase to the second floor. She poked her head into Harry's room and was greeted by the sight of her friend and Rumple both standing in front of a large floor-to-ceiling mirror scrutinizing Rumple's latest choice of outfit.

"But I can't even see my shoes!" Harry's manservant protested, peering down.

"I do rather think that is the point," Harry agreed convivially.

"Not seeing my shoes? How could that *possibly* be the point? I just bought these shoes. They cost the equivalent of an entire month's pay."

"No, I mean the point is the fashionability of it all." Harry waved his arms around. "Although I do wonder if I am over-paying you. All in all though, smashing. Don't you agree, Lillie?"

Lillie took in the trousers in question. There was something to be said for Rumple's current dissatisfaction. His shoes were nowhere to be seen under the enormous, ballooned Oxford bags. They were baggy to the point of ridiculousness.

"I'm interrupting," she said carefully, not wanting to fan the flames of their disagreement.

"Balderdash! Come in, come in," Harry urged.

"I don't understand..." she started, then thought the better of it.

"They've gone and bloody banned plus fours, have you heard?" Harry asked.

By plus fours he was referring to the ever-popular knicker-bockers—the pants that fell four inches below the knee and were so adored by the general male population of Oxford University students.

"I hadn't, no."

"Since when does the dean's office have a better sense of fashion than a twenty-two year old, I ask you. Anyway, these are all the rage now..." He waved in an offhand way at Rumple's pants.

"Meant as a protest, no doubt." Lillie raised a doubtful eyebrow.

"Oh." Harry seemed surprised. "Do you think so?" He scratched at his chin as though he were considering it.

"Harry, what *is* going on?"

"He's got me going in," Rumple answered with some reluctance. "*Undercover.*"

Lillie fought the urge to laugh out loud. How could he possibly be undercover in pants that screamed for attention? "In where?"

"Isn't it obvious?" Harry asked.

"Harry, other than those preposterous trousers, nothing here is obvious."

Harry shot her a look to suggest she was undermining his authority. "Into the lion's den, the dragon's lair, the deep dark belly of the underworld."

"Still not obvious, Harry."

He gave up, exasperated. "Well honestly, Lillie, it should be apparent by now. We are masquerading as Oxford students wanting to get someone to write a paper for us. Rumple, I do rather think you might consider something along the lines of, say...the epistemological foundation of metaphysics?"

Rumple gave his employer a blank look that Lillie thought about seconding. "Is that so, sir?"

"Certainly. You must not only look the part but have the substance to back it up."

"I do rather think it would be the substance that is lacking, presumably, if one is looking for one's paper to be written for them," Lillie interjected.

"Perhaps, perhaps," Harry mused. "What are you doing here anyway? I've been so distracted that I haven't asked."

Lillie fought the urge to blurt out her current predicament with Daniel, the intruders in her cottage, and the dead man as a result. But the less said about it all, the better. "I need you to accompany me back to Hanwell. Petters has had some tragic news: an officer of his was stabbed while on duty last night. He's passed away."

Harry's eyes widened like marbles. "You must be joking. Here? In Oxford?"

"Unfortunately I'm quite serious. Yes, here. And I wouldn't be at all surprised if it is related to our other murders, you see the officer had his eyes removed."

Harry visibly recoiled.

"An eye for an eye," Rumple said thoughtfully.

"Something like that, yes." Lillie thought briefly of Daniel and the horrendous scene in her cottage the night previous. The seventeenth-century philosopher Thomas Hobbes had once described life as 'nasty, brutish and short'—something she was increasingly beginning to believe, despite her nature to be optimistic.

"Ghastly news," Harry said solemnly. "I don't know *what* is going on but all this in our village? It has me terribly on edge. I've taken to sleeping with a firearm and Constance has finally gotten what she's always wanted, to be able to roam the estate at night searching out bandits and thieves."

Lillie thought about the welcome she'd gotten from the Irish Wolfhound just moments ago. Harry was mistaken if he thought his hound had anything even remotely resembling guard dog instincts; she was a complete pushover.

Harry continued. "Although I'd love to help, Lillie, I just can't possibly do it. Hanwell is just not my cup of tea."

"Harry don't be ridiculous. You know Petters can't possibly make a day trip now, and it's just one day. Say you'll come." If she was honest with herself, Lillie didn't want to revisit the place alone. It terrified her as much as it did Harry and having him along would certainly shore up her confidence.

"You've never been one to take no for an answer, have you?" Harry turned back to Rumple and began fiddling with the waist of the pants. He looked like a disgruntled seamstress and Rumple his reluctant mannequin.

"No. I haven't. Tomorrow afternoon then?"

"Only if I can have Rumple wait outside with the car—if only to spring us when that creepy Administrator Harris sees something so psychologically disturbing in me that he wants to have me admitted. We'll go after Rumple and I investigate the cheating."

"Thank you, Harry. Now, where I can I find Primrose?"

"Your house, of course. She can't seem to be kept away from that charming baby of yours."

"You've got a message." Today's secretary was a woman in her sixties with a low chignon and an impeccably tailored skirt and blouse combination. She was as thin as a stick and Lillie wondered if she ever ate a thing. She had half a mind to offer her half of the dried cherry scone she had just picked up from her favourite bakery. "You've just missed her." The woman added.

"Who?" Lillie asked, resisting the urge to dip into the parchment paper and start picking off the corners to eat. She should have taken Harry up on his offer of brunch.

"The woman who came in asking for you, obviously. Strange bird, that one."

Lillie wondered at the secretary's bluntness, it was just her first day after all. "Strange how?"

"Too tall and too abrupt to have good manners, for starters. Not to mention the nervous way she let her eyes dart around the room. As skittish as a cat in a puddle."

Lillie retrieved the bit of paper the message had been scrawled on and nodded her thanks.

"I'll be making coffee for the office in fifteen minutes," the secretary continued as she walked away. "But I don't serve it. Come to the kitchen if you'd like a cup."

Lillie waved her thanks and thought how much Jeremy would love the new recruit. She was as abrupt and matter-of-fact as he was. Had someone taken over the hiring? It seemed to be a daily occurrence around the newspaper.

She pulled out her desk chair and sat down, dropping her leather bag to the floor beside her and unfolding the message, which read: *Reporters need to report the news, especially when it concerns our women. You've been remiss, and this is a warning. We don't plan to give another.*

Lillie stared down at the scratched writing and reread it. The killer perhaps? But what was the 'we'? Or was it completely unrelated? It wasn't signed. She felt herself grow cold with trepidation. Was she next? They'd already harmed Jeremy and she was the lead crime reporter after all, why should she be immune? It was the last thing she wanted to bother Jeremy with and no doubt he was still pleading his case to the doctor at the hospital.

She picked up her bag off the floor and stood up. She'd have to report it to the police.

38

LILLIE

Oxford Police Station was as busy as Lillie had ever seen it. The death of one of their own had catapulted the regular officers into action and by the looks of it, Felix had also pulled in an army of specialists to help with the search for Officer Hicks's killer. They were easy to spot amongst the fray, their dark, pressed suits announcing their superiority as surely as an Etonian necktie would in the public realm. It was a bold move to murder anyone in cold blood, but a police officer was just that much more reckless.

The station secretary was buzzing around the reception desk, alternating between answering the constant ringing of the switchboard and fetching coffee and sandwiches for the personnel. She glanced up at Lillie when she entered and held up one finger to let her know she'd be right with her. Lillie took a seat on one of the unforgiving scalloped chairs and waited.

It was nearly six o'clock and she hadn't been home all day. She wondered how things were with Nanny and Lola and silently thanked the stars that Lola was just a baby and wouldn't register the things she had seen last night. She shuddered, asking herself if she could really expect to make a life with Daniel—and what would he do now? Petters had made it clear that while he wouldn't arrest him, at least not yet, he also wouldn't tolerate a wanted criminal on his turf. It ultimately meant Daniel would have to go; either that or he would have to stay hidden in the shadows. And wouldn't they just send others for him? Whoever 'they' were. Whatever he was mixed up in now threatened them all, but if she knew Daniel, and she was beginning to, she knew he wouldn't let what happened last night be the end of it.

"Miss Mead, good evening." Jeremiah had wandered into the station with his leashed badger while she was lost in her thoughts.

"Hello, young man." Lillie smiled at the company. Jeremiah had grown into a charming and healthy teenage boy in the time he'd been living with Petters. When Felix had found him at the orphanage over a year ago he had been not only as thin as a rail but also as shy as a cricket. "Terrible news for the police force today."

"Yes. I just brought Pa some sandwiches." He held up a wrinkled paper bag and flopped down in the seat next to her. "Any news?"

"Not that I've heard, but it looks as though they've pulled out all the stops. Your dad has every expert under the sun here."

"About time. If it's related to the rowers and the pub owner's murders then I suppose it'll be like killing two birds with one stone. Assuming they find him. Or her..." He paused, thinking. "What are you doing here?"

"Oh." Lillie never liked to involve the boy in police matters, he was too young and impressionable. "Just some routine business I'd like to see Felix about."

The secretary gave her a wave from behind the counter and

Lillie stood. "I won't be long with him then it's your turn." She tapped him on the nose and noticed him blush.

Felix's office was as neat as it always was when she entered, but the man behind the desk looked as though he'd been through the trenches.

"Anything?"

"Not yet," he answered. He caught the look on her face. "What've you got?"

Lillie handed him the message that had been left for her at the newspaper. He flicked it open and read it through. When he was finished he took off his glasses and looked straight at her. "I'll keep it for analysis. Anything new in your search for the missing story?"

"A drowning in London, a cheating scandal at the university, and a franchise equality rally. Take your pick. Of course it could also be none of those things. I can't tell you how difficult it is to look for something that actually doesn't exist!"

"I can imagine." Felix glanced up at one of his officers who was leaning against the open door.

"Sir, situation report in ten minutes," he said.

"Good," Felix replied.

"I'll let you get to it; Jeremiah is outside with your dinner."

Felix nodded. "Be careful, Lillie. If this is the same person, they've got you in their sights. When are you scheduled to visit Hanwell?"

"Tomorrow afternoon."

"Good, I want details immediately upon your return."

Felix gathered up his clipboard and made his way from the office, forgetting to say goodbye in his haste.

BY THE TIME Lillie arrived back home at Orchard Cottage Nanny had dinner on the table in the main house and was fussing with Lola in the tub.

"It's just there, my love," she called from the bathroom, then said something inaudible, presumably to Lola.

Lillie plopped down, dropping her bag on the scrubbed kitchen floor and for a split second had visions of the dead man lying there. She wondered if Daniel was around. She'd spotted two discreet but formidable-looking men on the way in and knew they were her latest security guards. It wasn't the first time she'd had protection; Petters had routinely put officers on her house depending on what story she was working on at any given time, but this time things felt different.

She finished nanny's delicious roast chicken and green salad and took the plates over to the sink to wash them. Staring out the window into the garden she wondered if the security men had eaten anything. Spying the remainder of the chicken in a pot still on the stove, she pulled a freshly baked loaf of bread out of the bread box, courtesy of Nanny White, and set to work slicing a few pieces to make them a couple of sandwiches. Then she put the kettle on to boil, fetched a large wooden tray and loaded it up with dinner, tea and a couple of plums from the orchard. She quietly let herself out the back and padded across the garden with it. One of the men spotted her and she held it up to show him dinner. He gave her a quick wave of acknowledgement and placed it on one corner of the rock wall, then turned and headed back to the main house.

Lola had just emerged, swaddled in a buttercup yellow blanket, when she let herself back into the kitchen.

"Here she is," Nanny said, handing her over to Lillie's awaiting arms. "I'll just finish warming her bottle and this little babe is ready for bed."

"Thank you." Lillie snuggled her baby, kissing her nearly bald head and whispering sweet nothings to her as she carried her through to the living room. She gently settled on to the sofa with her and jiggled her gently, watching two tiny fists emerge from the blanket and swat at the air.

Nanny arrived with the warm bottle and gave it to her. "I see we have some company this evening," she broached carefully, referring to Daniel's men outside.

"They are a little obvious, aren't they?" Lillie gently gave the bottle to Lola who started suckling on it immediately, her eyes fluttering as she tried to stay awake.

"It's none of my business, but there must be good reason for them to be here."

"There is, I'm afraid." Lillie attempted to cover up the real reason by adding, "I work on some dangerous assignments. It's par for the course, really."

"Of course it is. Nice enough fellows, they are too," Nanny finished neatly. "I gave them lunch and I'll be sure to see to it they are fed. I'll say goodnight then."

Lillie smiled up at her, feeling the exhaustion at the whole situation creep into her body. Sometimes she wondered at her own ability to handle the life she'd chosen to lead—her job, Daniel, saying goodbye to her fiancé Jack. "Thank you, for everything."

With that the woman left the room and headed back to her cottage for the night. Lillie sighed, gazing down at her baby who was nearly asleep. She heard the click of the kitchen door, and assumed it was Nanny leaving, but a moment later Daniel was standing in the living room.

Lillie felt the same surge of excitement she always had when she first laid eyes on him. That, and the feeling of coming home. She knew then and there, in that moment, that she didn't ever want to live without him.

As though he was reading her thoughts, Daniel silently moved through the room and lifted the sleeping baby from Lillie's arms, cradling her to his chest.

"I was just about to put her to bed," Lillie said, watching them. His face had taken on the most gentle expression and she found the contrast with the Daniel of the previous evening unsettling.

"I can fix it," he said softly, changing the conversation and being careful not to wake the baby in his arms.

"I assume by 'it' you mean the situation you find yourself in." Lillie felt her blood begin to boil. "You knowingly came here with them following you, did you not?" Not waiting for him to answer, she continued, barely checking her rage. "I have a *baby*, Daniel. How could you put us in this kind of danger?"

He dropped his head.

"How do you plan to 'fix it', as you say?" she asked, frowning.

"I'll have to go back—for a time."

She hated to think of him leaving, as furious as she was. "And what? Kill them all?"

He gave her a firm look to suggest she was being ridiculous. "I hardly think that would be possible, or necessary."

She waited for him to explain.

"It'll be a contingent who want me back in, it's more about control of its members than it is about anything else." He ran his hand over his short hair.

"I'm confused," Lillie started. "You can't leave on your own accord?"

"Not really, no."

"It's a life sentence?"

"Something like that." He rocked Lola gently.

Lillie got up from the sofa and began to pace the small living room. It was insanity. Surely now he was on the other side of the world they should leave him alone. He was hardly a threat to anyone while in England.

"How long will you be gone," she asked him, finding herself dreading his response. Would he even ever return?

He sidestepped her question, instead lifting his eyes from

the baby and meeting hers. "I can't tell you how sorry I am you had to witness that," he said softly.

Lillie nodded, curbing her frustration with him, and without another word she took Lola from his arms and headed up the stairs to bed.

39

The Christ Church Boat Club was located on a muddy edge of the Isis, the name given to the Thames river where it met Oxford and meandered through the countryside. Consisting of a collection of barges, their long low-slung bodies floating just off the shore and accessed by a series of wooden gangway ramps, the club was in the initial stages of set-up for the Oxford City Royal Regatta, a pre-Michaelmas term set of races that a few of the colleges competed in. The upper level of the first barge had been tented in white duck cloth, with official invite spectator chairs placed in neat rows behind the iron-grilled railings which faced the water. On race day, the general public would be lined far along the river banks, their feet damp and trousers seeping with wet as they cheered on their house of choice.

Underneath the spectator chairs was a lower floor that housed the various bars and house headquarters for the rowers and official invitees. A succession of white gothic windows, their upper sections pushed open to the night air, lined the entire length of each barge giving the entire structure a noble impression that would have been lacking otherwise.

I'm not sure we'll find him here at this hour, she protested as they neared the first gangway, the stillness of the river ensuring it remained nearly stationary as they descended onto the barge.

"Race day is Sunday. There isn't any doubt he'll be here. If not tonight then every other night until the event. The crew always works evenings setting up, you know this."

She didn't look sure and neither of them wanted to argue. They were closing in on the fifth. The others weren't really guilty, per se—the reporter just needed a reminder, for example—but these five were the reason they were here. Of course there were periphery players, this much was certain, but it was the core group who needed eradicating. For the good of the world.

Don't forget the chief, she reminded.

"How could I?" The big prize was the ringleader of them all, although he would have to wait until the bitter end—as per their plan.

The barges were softly lit from inside and the two of them could hear the shuffle of feet from inside the middle one. They crept towards it, hopping from the first barge to the next one along the outside walkway. They peered inside the windows and saw a crew of four young men who appeared to be doing more drinking than setting up. Their laughter echoed off the walls of the barge and reverberated outside. One of them was standing on a table doing some sort of an impression while the other three exploded into fits, hollering for more.

She pointed to one of the men. *Isn't that him?*

It had been so long they really had to look hard to be sure. "I believe so."

We'd better get it right, she insisted.

In the darkness she had begun to glow white in pieces. A wave of her hand, a flutter of hair. The wind had picked up and it blew her fine locks across her face. There had used to be freckles across her cheeks but for some reason they were absent tonight. As though she had grown out of them with each murder.

"Of course we will get it right, it's just a matter of being sure and then somehow getting to him."

They continued to watch the scene inside. The men had broken up and were continuing with whatever chores each were tasked to do. Their target was stacking glasses behind a bar, another was setting up tables. The two others were hanging house banners along the walls, laughingly putting them at haphazard angles and telling inappropriate stories while they did so.

Like a bunch of schoolchildren, she frowned her disapproval. *Nothing seems to affect them.*

They watched their target closely, willing him to break off from the group. He had moved on from glasses to bottles and he lifted a crate of them onto the bar and began to unload them.

"There's more outside," One of the men called to him. "Can't have enough bloody beer for Magdalen," he quipped, referring to one of the colleges.

"I'll get it," their target answered, finishing with the crate and carelessly tossing it to the floor with a clatter.

He was a good-looking bloke, there wasn't any denying that, and they wondered why he'd needed to do what he had done.

It's not about that, she said, once again being the mind reader that she was. *It's about power and control.*

"I suppose so, yes."

The target had moved out from behind the makeshift bar and was saying something to the two who were hanging the banners. The three of them erupted into laughter and the one on the ladder nearly toppled over.

Too bad, she said, flicking back her ghostly hair as he righted himself. She was getting into it now.

"Quickly, move to the side so he doesn't see you." Although no one seemed to ever see her.

They hurried around the corner of the barge and noticed the stack of full crates that had been piled by the gangway. Presumably those were what he was coming for. They passed by them and hid in the shadow of the building. The water lapped below them. They heard the door slam at the front of the barge and the sound of footsteps as their target moved around the side of the building. He was nearly on top of them within seconds and even though they had role-played their moves to precision, reality rarely reflected even the best planning. He had leaned over to heave one of the crates onto his shoulder and as he did so their world seemed to move in slow motion. She clapped her hands in glee as they hurled themselves on to his back knocking him off balance. The crate fell from his arms to the ground and while they braced themselves for the smash of glass it didn't come as expected, the crate instead cradling the bottles and shielding them from the fall.

Their target, however, fell forward and smashed his face on the edge of the wooden crate. It took him a second to right himself, and as he rolled over to face his attacker they managed to plunge their well-used knife directly into his heart.

The stunned look on his face told them he didn't recognize either of them. One more stab to ensure he was really dead, although his blank eyes now looking skyward was enough evidence even for the meek.

Will you really take that? she asked, incredulous.

"We said we would, didn't we?"

She nodded her agreement and they got right to work. When they'd finished they dragged the Oxford University rower's body to the side of the barge and heaved him over into the river.

It was a good thing he was already dead.

40

HARRY

They'd opted for a reversal of roles the next morning, and as Harry negotiated the Rolls Royce Silver Ghost carefully along the narrow, winding road on the outskirts of Oxford, he wondered if they hadn't made a grave error.

"Mind the stone wall," Rumple barked violently from the backseat, as Harry overcorrected rather abruptly.

"Must you address me like that!" he snapped back at his manservant, not taking his eyes off the road ahead of him while instantly regretting the lack of practice he'd taken on polishing his skills before they set out.

"I was concerned about the car, sir." A ruffle of fabric let Harry know he had changed his position behind him and had become instantly more attentive.

"Yes, thank you, but I had it just bloody fine without your interference," Harry scolded.

"It's just there, in that house, do you see it?" Rumple leaned forward and pointed through the windscreen at a slender, ivy-clad stone house with a tight drive that took them over a moss-covered canal. It had a small gravel courtyard in front, in which were parked a number of bicycles in a disorganized fashion. "I don't suppose many students arrive being chauffeured," he noted, reflectively.

"Mm," Harry agreed. "I do rather think that may have been an oversight, yes." He slowed the great car and evaluated the turn. "It'll be tight but here it goes..."

"It would be quite an entrance to end up in the water, sir."

"May I remind you I worked in logistics during the war, Rumple. I think I can get across a drainage canal without too much difficulty," Harry huffed, annoyed.

"Yes sir, although you were behind a desk and not actually in the field."

Must he point out every deficiency? Harry wondered. Although to be honest, admittedly it was true. The war for Harry had consisted of meetings where little was achieved and weekly drinks parties meant to 'shore up' the troops. Harry turned the great car over the bridge and entered the courtyard at a snail's pace. They crept up to the house and parked near the front door.

"I'll just wait here then, shall I?" Harry said hopefully. "You wouldn't bring your chauffeur in with you, surely."

"Oh, no sir. I think you'd better be there too. Especially since you know exactly who we are asking around about."

Harry groaned and got out of the car, then came around the side facing the house and opened Rumple's door with ceremony.

They made their way to the front door, glancing around at their surroundings, and knocked. It all looked neat as a pin and the house had the air of perfect respectability. They door was answered by a meek-looking young woman of indeterminate age who showed them into a study near the back of the house. Although a dark room, comprised of small windows and great hulking book cases, it was nonetheless quite pleasant. Someone had thought to adorn the side tables with fresh flowers and all the lamps were lit. They could hear a few voices outside the room as they settled into their chosen seats to wait.

"Seems quite a nice place, really ," Rumple remarked. "Are you sure you've got the right location?"

"Of course I do," Harry snapped. "I confirmed twice and called ahead for an appointment, they are expecting us. I was quite surprised they were here during the holidays but I suppose there is enough work to keep them going all year. It does rather make one wonder just how much cheating goes on on a regular basis." He regarded Rumple. "You do have your request then, don't you?"

"The metaphysical something-or-other..." Rumple searched his pockets, pulling out a piece of crumpled paper. Harry frowned his disapproval at his manservant's cavalier note-taking. "Ah, here it is. Yes, I am prepared."

"Hardly," Harry scoffed.

The door to the study opened and a tall, lean man who looked to be about thirty years old entered the room.

"Hello, Mr Wallace?"

It was the name Harry had given when he'd made the appointment but he'd forgotten to mention it to Rumple.

After a moment of a blank stare Rumple caught on. "Yes, yes," he answered.

"Ah, good. John Smith. How can I help you today?"

Was he serious? *John Smith*? An alias if Harry had ever heard one.

"I was hoping for some help on a paper," Rumple started.

John Smith sized him up. Admittedly, the whole thing, including the trousers, looked ridiculous. Rumple was far too old to be an Oxford student.

"For his nephew," Harry put in, clearing his throat while changing tactic.

"I see." John Smith looked back and forth between them.

Rumple nodded his confirmation and handed Smith the

crumpled paper he was holding. Smith read it and then nodded. "Word count?"

"Oh, ten thousand or under," Harry confirmed, pulling a number out of thin air. "Is that a possibility?"

"When do you need it?"

"Ten days." Rumple said.

"The class it's for?" Smith asked.

"Philosophy." Harry answered.

"Fine."

Smith was the can-do sort and Harry wondered if this would be the time to discuss money.

"I need something a little extra with it," Harry started carefully.

Smith looked as though nothing Harry said would surprise him. "I'm all ears."

He leaned in closer and Harry reached into the pocket of his chauffeur uniform to retrieve a large wad of bills. He then pushed them across the table to Smith.

"I'm looking for some information on your client list."

Smith looked at them both through narrowed eyes. "I take it we can forget the philosophy paper, then?"

"Something like that," Harry confirmed, but he could already see they were going to get what they came for.

41

SUPERINTENDENT FELIX PETTERS

O fficer Hale was already at the river's edge when Felix arrived three miles downstream from the Christ Church Boat Club later that morning with a mug of coffee in hand, having spilled half of it in the police car. He'd already called another investigator from a neighbouring territory, a woman in her fifties who was cloaked in an apron, gloves and a sunhat. He couldn't decide if she looked as though she belonged on a beach in Cornwall or behind a stove in a kitchen. As it was, she was one of the best investigators he'd ever worked with, and he'd taken to calling her in for help when he was finding himself baffled on a particular case—as he was now.

"What've you got?" he asked, taking a large sip of coffee while simultaneously swatting at a couple of gnats who were biting at his forearms. He'd rolled up his sleeves as the temperatures crept into the nineties and he wiped his brow as he peered over her shoulder at the covered body. She dropped to her knees and began creeping around the grass near it as though she were looking for grasshoppers.

"Male, early twenties, by all accounts healthy."

"What are you looking for?" he asked.

"His missing penis," she answered without looking up.

Petters choked hard on his coffee. He coughed to clear his throat. "I'm sorry?" Surely he hadn't heard her correctly.

"Yes. A surprise to me too," she agreed.

"Is that the cause of death?" How gruesome.

"Not likely. We'll have to confirm with the coroner, but it appears these two stab wounds to the chest seem to have finished him off first." She waved in the general direction of the sheeted figure as though he could see the injuries through the fabric.

Petters looked over at Officer Hale and motioned for him to join them.

"Who called it in?" Petters questioned him.

"A couple of gents who had come to the river early this morning for fishing. Said he had washed up on shore just there." The officer pointed to a reedy area of marsh where the long grass had been flattened.

"Don't supposed they saw anyone else at the time?"

"I don't think so, no."

Petters frowned at his officer. "You don't *think* so? Did you actually ask."

"I believe so, yes."

"Honestly, Hale, that sounds like the most dithering answer you've ever given me. Go back to them immediately and find out." Petters turned his attention back to the woman crawling on the ground. "Any luck?" he asked her.

"I don't think it's here," she answered from the grass below.

It was their sixth victim, Petters reflected. A head, an arm, two eyes, an ear, a finger and now this. A *penis*. What was left? Or more accurately, who was left?

"I'll have a sweep of the area done this morning," he assured her, swallowing the last of his coffee. I'm heading back to the station to organize the roster now.

The investigator nodded, straightening her sunhat and getting up.

"So it's sexual in nature," Petters confirmed with her.

"Possibly," she agreed. "But not definitely."

"I would hope by the time I get back to the station someone has reported him missing so at least we can get a quick identification." Petters looked up and down the river. He could have been thrown off a boat, he supposed, and have come from anywhere.

"I wouldn't be surprised if he's an Oxford student."

Petters hadn't yet pulled the sheet back but he leaned down and did so now. "The clothes," he agreed. The trousers were gone but from the waist up he was dressed as a typical rower would be—a white, v-necked sweater, now soiled with muddy water. "I'll start there," Petters agreed, turning back towards the police car.

IT WAS NEARLY noon when Felix reached the police station and most of his day staff were already out on rounds. Their receptionist had already left for lunch, so Petters headed to the station kitchen and set to work making a large pot of coffee himself. While it brewed, he headed back to reception and flicked through the small stack of overnight messages. If there was something urgent, it would have been immediately handed to the overnight skeleton crew of officers. Otherwise, whatever it was would wait until morning and remain in the follow-up box. There was a report about a noise complaint from a high street apartment, one about a stolen cow, another about a vandalized car, and one from the Christ Church Boat Club noting one of their crew hadn't returned from a supply run. Had anyone followed up? He checked the time at the top of the message. One o'clock in the morning. No doubt the switchboard operator had just assumed it was a drunken student who had misplaced his friend.

Petters headed back to the kitchen with the message in hand, poured himself a coffee and then headed through the main room to see if he could catch anyone at their desks. A junior officer was eating his bagged lunch at his desk.

"See this?" Petters waved the message at him. "Missing Oxford student last night about one o'clock."

"Uh." The officer looked as nervous as a cornered fox. "I didn't, no."

"Did you check them when you came in?"

"I didn't sir, no. I thought Marshall did."

"And he probably thought you did." Petters handed the officer the message. "Follow it up, immediately."

"Yes, sir." The junior officer dropped his lunch onto the desk and retrieved his uniform coat.

Petters returned to his office and pulled out a stack of case files he had been gathering of the past three years of cases. Whatever was going on had something to do with a past grievance; he was sure of it. Three dead students, a dead pub worker, and a murdered police officer. He had been a fool not to see the connection to the police earlier. All this time Lillie had been looking for an event they *hadn't* reported on. What if it had to do with police negligence? Or worse. Felix hadn't been with the Oxford department long enough to know it's history, but it was about time he educated himself.

He sat down behind his desk and got to work.

42

LILLIE

Hanwell Insane Asylum looked much as it had the other day when Lillie and Harry had visited. Today the sun had disappeared behind a thick layer of cloud, casting a dull hue over the entire institution and chasing the wandering patients inside. They lingered now in groups of two or three, the inhospitable hallways their refuge from their prison-like rooms.

"Another dead—and a missing genital." Harry shuddered as they walked towards the administrator's office. "I'm beginning to wonder if Oxford has become the setting for a Shelley novel. Honestly Lillie, I don't think Constance is nearly up to the task of guarding Tynesmore. I'm considering adding a couple of Doberman Pinchers to my growing collection of animals. I know of an exceptional German breeder who has been trying to get his dogs into England for years." He moved out of the way to avoid a patient who was babbling to himself while wandering down the insipid stone hallway, incessantly knocking on the walls. "And what about you? Have you considered some sort of protection for you and Lola?"

Lillie thought about the two men in the garden who

Nanny had fed breakfast to that morning. Daniel had certainly ensured that not only were they safe from the Oxford murderer, but also from anyone who was coming for him.

"I'm not worried about us, Harry." They rounded the corner and stood before the office.

"I despise this place," Harry grumbled.

"As do I; let's get this done quickly," she agreed.

They'd left Rumple in the car outside the front gates. Harry had told him in no uncertain terms to be ready to flee at a moment's notice and furthermore if they weren't out within the hour to come looking for them. Lillie had laughed at him and told him not to be so silly.

They wandered into the administrator's bank of offices and took a seat.

"He won't be long," his secretary assured them over her half-moon glasses.

Harry dusted off the armrests on his matching unforgiving chair. "Is it really so difficult to obtain comfortable furniture? No wonder everyone in here is insane. One would only need to visit this ghastly building once, and have a seat for five minutes, to lose one's faculties. I'm already feeling as though I'm at my wits' end." He glanced nervously around the office. "I don't suppose I could get a whiskey?"

"Try to keep it all together, Harry. We won't be here long," Lillie reprimanded.

Harry breathed in and out heavily, trying to calm himself. He pulled at the collar of his shirt as though it had begun to choke him.

After a few agonizing minutes of watching Harry slowly but certainly break into a sweat, the secretary announced, "The administrator will see you now, Miss Mead."

Harry jumped up and launched forward as though he were in the starting gates at Newmarket. He was at the door to the private office before Lillie could even gather her bag off the floor.

"Ah, we meet again." The administrator stood and came around from his desk to shake their hands. "I expect you've got more questions for your article on the asylum?" He gave Lillie a look to suggest that if she didn't, she certainly better come up with some very quickly.

"I do," she played along. A male ego such as the administrator's was a tremendously uncomplicated thing to deal with. "I've just finished the first draft and plan to submit it tomorrow. It's really a very good story, if I do say so myself. I wouldn't be at all surprised if it were to be picked up by a few of the nationals," she lied.

"Wonderful." He clapped his hands with pleasure. "It's never an easy thing to secure public funding for our programmes—no doubt because they are so avant guard—any sort of press we can get is infinitely helpful."

Lillie immediately regretted her lies. Putting the administrator's ego aside, she decided she would do the story after all.

"So," she began carefully, pulling her notebook from her bag. "I'd like to fill out my understanding a little more of the Oxford University programmes that were undertaken here."

"Yes, yes of course. How can I help?" The administrator leaned forward across his desk.

"Let's start with the art programme. You've given me a broad understanding of the methodology behind the paintings, the use of body parts et cetera." She fought back her disgust at the memory of their conversation.

"It has produced some exceptional work. We've begun to create a display wall in the south corridor and I have some notable interest from a small gallery in London to house an exhibit. It's possible it may even become a travelling collection —this particular gallery has connections throughout the continent."

"I see." Lillie jotted down a few notes.

Harry shifted beside her but remained quiet, taking instead to staring longingly out the window of the administrator's office.

"When we were last here, you gave me a list of the Oxford students who participated in that art programme."

"Yes." The administrator cupped his enormous hands and placed them on the desk, giving her his full attention. "And have you followed up with any of them? A couple of quotes on their experience here at Hanwell would go a long way to filling out your article and giving the programme, and ultimately the institution, the validity it so deserves."

"Mm," Lillie agreed, nodding. "Would it be possible to get a list of patients who also participated in the programme here?"

"Of course. And you must come and see their work. I'll take you to the south corridor and you can see them for yourself. There were about thirty of them—obviously some are far more talented than others, but all in all it is quite an interesting collection."

"Yes, I'd like to see that."

Harry cleared his throat. "But we haven't got much time..." he started.

"Enough to see the collection," Lillie insisted. The more interest she showed, the more Administrator Harris was likely to cooperate. "If we could get the list first, though?" she prodded. "I'd like to be able to reference the artists as we go."

"Of course, my dear." The administrator heaved his huge bulk out of his chair and headed to the door. He pulled it open and boomed his request to his secretary.

She returned moments later with a list which she handed to Lillie.

"Oh, thank you." Lillie took the copy, perused it quickly, and then tucked it inside her bag.

"So, shall we?" Administrator Harris said to them, standing once again and heading towards the open door.

As they headed out into the corridor they heard the distant sound of howling from somewhere deep in the recesses of the building.

"Dear God," Harry muttered under his breath, increasing his pace.

Lillie matched it step for step. The sooner they were out of this place the better.

43

SUPERINTENDENT FELIX PETTERS

"We've got a missing persons report for Dean Milquist. It was just filed an hour ago."

Superintendent Felix Petters stood in full uniform in the drawing room at Tynesmore. The evening breeze was coming through the French doors leading to the patio and Rumple had placed a cocktail of some indistinguishable colour into his hands. Felix held it now as though it were a baby someone had just thrust, unwanted, into his arms.

"I'm not staying, I've got a car out—" he attempted, but Rumple appeared not to hear him. Instead, Harry's manservant floated back to his place behind the bar and began mixing his next drink with some vehemence in a sterling silver shaker, effectively drowning out their conversation for the moment.

"We do try to humour him," Harry said above the din. "He seems to be on this *cocktails are all the rage* kick at the moment and after the day we've just had at Hanwell, I don't want to dissuade him."

Lillie frowned and pushed her hair off her forehead. "Is it possible he just went birding?"

"The dean? I don't think so, no."

"Who reported him missing?" she asked, perplexed.

"When he didn't show up for work today, his office called around to his house and his wife said he'd left for work hours ago. He never made it in and he didn't come home for dinner. Apparently he never misses one."

"Certainly not with that girth, no. He isn't the youngest man. Perhaps he just tootled off on some errand and lost track of time," Harry put in. "I once had an uncle who was constantly wandering off. My aunt once found him in a brothel this side of..."

"Thank you, Harry," Lillie interrupted. "But I agree with you, he isn't young, no." Lillie scratched at her forehead. "But he's hardly at the stage of wandering off. He's still as sharp as a nail."

"Anyway, with the current climate as it is, it's something to be concerned about. Had we not just had five murders and a kidnapping in this community, I mightn't be so hyper-vigilant about it."

"Where will you start looking?" Lillie asked. "I mean, have you anything to go on?"

"Not really," Petters adjusted his uniform jacket.

Lillie interjected. "There's the Oxford City Royal Regatta this weekend, you know. The dean's absence would be a huge blow. Christ Church College is not only entered, but it's favoured to win. Not to mention that nearly every public address is meant to be given by him."

"Is that perhaps significant?" Harry asked. "Given the timing?"

"Someone kidnaps the dean, or worse, two days before the biggest athletic event on the Oxford summer calendar and the university has a number of teams entered? I should certainly say so," Lillie said.

Petters ran his hand over his scalp. "What've you learned today. Let's work backwards."

"Well, for starters Harry and Rumple found out some very interesting information from the academic paper and exam writers," Lillie said.

"I'm sorry?" Petters looked confused.

"The chaps that do the cheating for hire," Harry added for clarification.

"Oh yes, of course."

"Turns out," Harry started, "not only did they write a paper last year for Andrew Baker, but they also do work for other university students throughout England."

"I see." Petters clearly didn't see where the conversation was headed.

"I asked specifically about David Spool, among others. No record of Edwin Hastock, our first victim, by the way. Although they did supply a test a few years back to that rotten coxswain Will Andrews. Fitting really..."

"What about Spool?" Petters tried to steer Harry back.

"Oh right, yes. Well, interestingly when they looked him up they came back with an Adam Spool instead. I didn't dare correct them; Spool is hardly a common name so while at first I thought they might have just been confused about the first name I did let them run with it, in case I was missing something. Turns out this Adam Spool attends the London School of Medicine, or did so at that time. This was about eighteen months ago now."

"Go on," Petters urged.

"Right well, they had been hired by someone associated with Adam Spool, a family member although they had no record of *which* family member, to supply a medical school exam for Adam ahead of his formal sitting."

"And these...these cheating people just have such things lying around? I don't understand."

"Not quite, no. It is a complex operation they are running. They have contacts, or try to obtain contacts, in most major universities across the country. They then pay these contacts very handsomely for their efforts in stealing the most current tests for each subject. Apparently they don't bother with the smaller quizzes but instead focus on the final exams, which are in very high demand indeed, and people don't seem to mind paying top dollar for them. Of course there is also another arm of their business which employs essay writers who complete routine term papers in whatever subject the student might need." Harry took a long drink of his cocktail and leaned one arm against the fireplace mantle. "Not a bad business model actually. Certainly beats the racing—I lost a packet last year on a couple of fillies I bought at auction who turned out to be the most dismal prospects, not fit for pulling a milk cart much less qualifying for Ascot."

"But who would hire a stolen test for this chap and how is this related? Is it just a coincidence, the name Spool?"

"This we don't know, at least not yet," Lillie added. "However, having this information made our trip to Hanwell this afternoon a little more focused. We got the list of patients who were participating in David Spool's art programme and low and behold..."

"Adam Spool," Petters finished for her.

"Correct," Lillie answered. "The administrator hadn't put it together and when I pressed him towards the end of our meeting he seemed not to remember whether or not the two men had even interacted much less whether or not they were even related."

"So what was Adam Spool in Hanwell for? Is he actually mentally insane?" Petters queried.

"Well, it would seem so if he was there," Harry put in.

"We can't get his full medical records without a warrant," Lillie answered.

"That will take too much time," Petters said.

"As I thought, so I have another way." Lillie nodded at them. "We'll go and visit David Spool's parents."

Petters nodded his agreement and then gave her a calculating stare as though he was formulating a theory. "I don't supposed this Adam Spool is still at Hanwell?"

Lillie shook her head slowly. "He was released a month ago."

"And his current whereabouts?" Petters looked expectant.

"Well, that's just it. He didn't show up for his periodic medical check-up. As an outpatient, he is meant to be checking in with the Hanwell doctor every week for the first three months upon release." She paused and gave him a grave look. "Adam Spool is missing."

44

LILLIE

The Spools lived in a tidy but small brick terraced house on the outskirts of Wycombe, a market town set in the rolling landscape of the Chiltern Hills in Buckinghamshire. As Rumple pulled the Silver Ghost up in front of their cottage the following day, Lillie stared out at the ivory-trimmed windows and wondered how the Spools managed to afford to not only send David to Oxford, but to buy stolen exams—assuming they had done so.

"Scholarship, I would surmise. Either that or a rich relative." Harry said, reading her thoughts and looking out the window at the narrow cobblestoned road which the car had fairly easily managed to dominate with its hulking body. "You won't be able to leave it here, old chap," he called to the front seat.

Rumple shook his head in disagreement. "I'll circle round if need be but it hardly seems to be a well-travelled route, sir." He glanced around at the nearly empty neighbourhood as though to make his point, then cut the engine.

"Mm," Lillie agreed with Harry's former statement. "There must be some financial aid of some sort, although one shouldn't judge a book by its cover." Who knew how people managed the things they did. "I hope we catch someone at home." The windows of the house showed no sign of life.

They hadn't sent a message to the Spools asking to meet, preferring instead to arrive unannounced, mostly because they weren't sure about David and didn't want him anywhere near his parents while they interviewed them. Wycombe was an easy trip from Oxford and it wouldn't take much for David to show up.

Felix hadn't come with them. He was needed at the station now that their manhunt had expanded from the core of the city out into the countryside. He had officers stationed at all major routes in and out of the city and while there hadn't been any new information on the whereabouts of the dean before they left, Lillie was beginning to wonder if he would be found alive.

Lillie opened her door and slid out of the car with Harry following suit. The door to the Wycombe house was immaculately painted in a robin's egg blue and Lillie raised her hand to knock. It was answered by a small woman in her late forties with dark hair and a pair of reading glasses perched on the end of her nose. She was wearing a floral apron and had her hair pulled back into a neat, low bun.

"Good day," Lillie started. "You'll have to forgive our intrusion and I'm terribly sorry I didn't send a note ahead of time. I'm Lillie Mead and this is my associate Harry Green."

"Yes?" Mrs Spool had the confused look anyone might have when they found two unknown people on their doorstep.

"I work for an Oxford newspaper which has been covering the story of the recent murders there. Your son, David, has been extremely helpful in the police investigation and I wondered if I might be able to discuss some things with you."

"With me?" She was surprised. "Why me? I don't know a thing about it."

"It's just a routine follow-up for the newspaper. The piece

I'm working on is a comprehensive overview of what life is like for families who send their children to the university to study." Lillie smiled disarmingly. "We do these more in-depth pieces sometimes, usually for a weekend edition when people have time to delve into more complex stories and aren't just looking for headlines."

"It is a terrible thing that's happening there. It really is. I'm worried for my David."

"May we?" Lillie asked, motioning to the inside of the house. "It won't take more than about fifteen minutes."

"Yes, of course."

Mrs Spool stood back to allow Lillie and Harry inside, then turned and led them into a drawing room that was crammed with furniture. Lining the walls were oak hutches and book-shelves, in the middle of the room were a collection of small wooden side tables and stuffed between everything was a divan sofa and a couple of small upholstered chairs. Intricate lace curtains hung on wooden rods above a couple of windows that looked out on to a small, now parched, yard.

Harry gave Lillie a perplexed stare.

"My husband works in the furniture factory, you see," Mrs Spool clarified, seeing their surprise at the cluttered room. "Often he brings pieces home that have the odd blemish—a knot here or a crack there. Things that aren't suitable for sale."

"Ah, I see," Harry said, understanding. "Quite a handsome commode there." He pointed to a mahogany side table with two drawers. "I don't suppose he sells off these imperfect pieces? I daresay that little beauty would be quite an exceptional addition to my dressing room."

"Oh, certainly he does." She beamed her pride back at them. "And I work with lace." She motioned to the curtains while Lillie caught a brief wince on Harry's features. "So if there is anything I can make for you, please let me know."

"How lovely, just lovely." Harry looked around him and swallowed.

"Tell me," Lillie started, pulling a notebook out of her bag. "How is David enjoying his studies?"

"Oh, tremendously." Mrs Spool hopped up from her chair. "Can I offer you some tea?"

"No, thank you." Lillie wanted her interview to carry on uninterrupted. "What year is he in?"

"His fourth and final." The woman smiled. "Although I know he'd like to continue into a graduate programme if possible. It's just the cost, really, it's terribly expensive."

"Is he on a scholarship?"

"Yes, partially, and the remainder of his tuition was funded by an uncle of his, God rest his soul."

"Mm, yes," Harry agreed. "Where would one be if not for family." He flicked a bit of lint off one impeccably pressed trouser leg.

"Speaking of family, has David any siblings?" Lillie poised her pen over her notebook and didn't look up. The last thing she wanted was to seem as though she were fishing.

Mrs Spool shifted in her seat. The moment of pause was enough to tell them she was uncomfortable with the line of questioning. "He does, yes. A younger brother."

Lillie opened her mouth to ask his name, even though she all but knew it already, but was interrupted by the sound of the front door opening.

"Maeve, have you seen the size of the car out front?" called a voice from the foyer.

"In here," Mrs Spool answered, jumping up to greet him.

There was the sound of something being dropped and a few seconds later Mr Spool stood at the threshold of the drawing room.

"Oh," he said with surprise. "Hello. I'm Ronald Spool."

"Lillie Mead, from the *Oxford Daily Press* and this is my

associate, Harry Green." Lillie stood to shake his hand. "We've just come to interview you and Mrs Spool for a lifestyle piece we are doing about university life."

"I see..." Ronald Spool stood well over six feet tall and made the room look smaller and more cramped than it already was. He flicked his dark eyes between his wife and his guests.

"They've come to ask about David," Mrs Spool clarified in response to her husband's confused look.

"Yes." Lillie smiled. "And we were just asking about David's younger brother. Is he here in Wycombe?"

"He was, yes, until he went to the London School of Medicine," she answered proudly. Mr Spool shot his wife a warning look that Lillie immediately caught. "At least, until—" She broke off, realizing she'd said too much. "He had some upset," she finished.

"What type of upset?" Lillie prodded.

"Is that important to your article?" Mr Spool had yet to take a seat and he looked as though he might usher them out at any minute.

What was it they were hiding? Had whatever this 'upset' was caused their younger son to be admitted to Hanwell? Lillie found herself at a loss for words, mostly because she knew they were treading on less than solid footing.

"It's interesting," Harry began thoughtfully, filling up the awkward silence. "That the experiences of siblings can vary so greatly, isn't it? I for one have a completely different reality from my older brother and yet we are cut from the very same cloth— albeit his piece must've been somewhat broader, now that I think of it."

As though to put the whole issue to bed, Mrs Spool quickly added, "Oh, a friend of his passed away suddenly." She looked to her husband but he didn't meet her eye.

"Did it happen here in Wycombe?" Lillie asked.

"In Oxford," Mrs Spool answered. "A few years ago."

"And was it an accident?" Harry asked.

Neither of the Spools answered. Instead Mr Spool wandered back into the foyer and opened the front door. "Thank you for coming but we really have quite a bit of work to do today."

Lillie gave Harry a perplexed look and gathered her bag up off the floor. When the door had shut behind them and they were walking back to the car, she leaned in and whispered to Harry. "I'll investigate the dead friend. You go to the London School of Medicine and see if you can find out why Adam Spool left school."

"*Medical* school." Harry raised his eyebrows, ensuring she was getting the full implication of it.

Rumple was standing at the open passenger door while the long, low car idled beside the Spools front fence. He nodded to them as they approached.

"Yes," Lillie agreed, looking over her shoulder back to the house. She caught the glimpse of Mr Spool just as one delicate lace curtain dropped to cover the window.

45

LILLIE

"And just what are you doing here?" Lillie demanded.

She stood in the open doorway of Jeremy Winston's office at the *Oxford Daily Press* with her hands on her hips to illustrate her displeasure at his sudden reappearance.

"How many years' worth of stories have you pulled?" he asked from behind a stack of newspapers piled nearly high enough to completely obscure his diminutive size. She could just barely see the glint from one of the lenses of his glasses, as he ignored her original question.

"Eighteen months so far, but we'll need to go further. Does the hospital know where you are?"

"Don't be silly. Of course they do. I was released a couple of hours ago. Where've you been?"

"Wycombe. I went to visit David Spool's parents." She stepped into his office. "Interesting to say the least."

"Oh, and?"

"There are certainly some secrets there. Mostly around the younger brother, I think. Harry's gone to London to follow it up —apparently he attended a medical school there but didn't finish his degree. Anyway, when I know more I'll get you up to speed." She gave her boss a fond smile. He didn't look particularly well and the toll of the past surely weighed on him—he was thinner than he'd ever been, which was saying something on a chronically underweight man, and his eyes had lost the shine they'd once had. She hoped he'd eventually be back to himself but it wouldn't happen overnight.

"I see." Jeremy fiddled with his pencil.

"I'll get back to it then." Lillie hesitated. Did he want to tell her something? "Anything else?" she prodded.

"Do you remember a few years back there were some marches here in Oxford?"

"There are always marches about something or other, Jeremy; it's a university town after all. Which one, in particular?"

"The one I'm referring to was a rally demanding equal franchise. In July of 1921."

Lillie hadn't covered the story herself so it was unlikely she'd really remember the ins and outs of it. She stepped further into his office and took a seat across from his desk. "Is this something you now remember?"

Jeremy rubbed at his head. "No, *bloody hell*. I can't remember a thing about it but I've just found the story here; it's unusually brief from us, barely a mention really—and I can't figure out why there wasn't a follow-up to it. I've searched everything from July through to December of that year. Nothing at all."

"Would there be a follow-up? I mean, if most marches happen in the afternoon and they're over by nightfall, that's that. Why *would* the paper follow up? Unless—"

Jeremy flicked his pencil on to the desk and Lillie watched as it rolled across and dropped to the floor at his feet. She waited but he didn't pick it up.

"Unless something happened," Jeremy finished for her.

"Something more than just a protest. Someone got injured? Even killed?"

Jeremy nodded his agreement.

Lillie continued, "And then we would have reported on it in a follow-up piece. But if you don't remember anything like that happening why are you focused on this particular event?"

Jeremy swivelled in his chair and reached behind him, retrieving a leather-bound notebook that Lillie hadn't seen before.

"I've made myself some notes, or I did two summers ago."

Lillie stared at the book. "Where did that come from? I searched your whole office and never found it."

"It was at home. I don't keep it here. I retrieved it after the hospital hoping there would be something in it that might prod my memory. It isn't necessarily about work. I use it for every-thing—lists, things to do, that sort of thing—so I don't really know why I was even looking in it."

Lillie raised one eyebrow. "And?"

"And I've made a note to myself to interview the pub owner."

"Which pub owner? The murder victim?"

"Yes." He nodded gravely.

"In July of 21," Lillie confirmed. Jeremy nodded. "And you obviously don't remember if you did that or not."

"Exactly right."

"No follow-up notes in there? On the interview, I mean," Lillie asked.

"Not that I've recorded here, no."

"Well, it could have been for anything, Jeremy. Maybe the protest went by his doorway and you wanted a personal perspective piece. Or perhaps it was something to do with..." She stopped. The look on his face told her she was way off the mark.

"I wrote *rape*, here in the margin." He turned the book so she could see.

There it was in his chicken-scratch writing, barely readable but underlined twice.

Lillie nodded, quietly formulating and then reformulating a theory. "*If* you had interviewed the pub owner and *if* he knew something about a rape, you would have reported on it, Jeremy. It's you, after all! Of course you would have."

"Unless someone threatened me not to."

"Like who? And incidentally, you've been threatened more times than I can count; you don't back down very easily."

Jeremy nodded quietly but Lillie couldn't help but shake the memory of his demeanour the day she'd returned from France. He had been skittish. Something had spooked him that morning and though he couldn't now remember what it was, there was something in it, she was sure of it. Had someone from the past contacted him? Threatened him? Or had something happened in order to make him regret *not* printing the rape story? "I'll look for it in the other papers to see if there was anything in that month, or the following of the same year. Surely if that happened someone else would have reported it." Although even as she said it, Lillie had some doubts. If they hadn't reported on it and it was in their own town, it was unlikely anyone else had either.

Jeremy nodded solemnly as Lillie gathered up her bag and made her way from his office.

"JULY OF 1921?" Superintendent Felix Petters was sitting outside the Oxford Police Station on a low rock wall holding a teacup and the tail end of a leash.

"Yes. Jeremy said he'd made a note to himself about a possible rape following a franchise equality protest. He was to interview the pub owner but he can't remember, of course, whether he ever did." Lillie looked down at the small fox on the end of the leash. He had one front leg bandaged and he peered back at her through two dark eyes that spoke volumes. "Are you not worried he'll bite you?" she asked her friend.

"He's just a pup, and really quite gentle. Jeremiah found him in a leg-hold trap just outside the yard. Poor little fellow had tried to chew his own leg off."

"Horrible things. They should be outlawed," Lillie commiserated. She considered giving the animal a pat but thought the better of it.

Petters set his cup down on the stone wall and handed her the leash. "I'll just go ask Virginia to pull the files on the case, assuming there are any. It was before my time here in Oxford so it isn't something I would know much about."

While he was gone Lillie took up her place on the wall and studied her charge. He couldn't have weighed more than about fifteen pounds at the most, his front legs were jet black from the chest down and he had the most beautiful chestnut fur which ran lengthwise along his back. It looked as though someone had recently shampooed it and she smiled, imagining Jeremiah attempting to bathe the creature. The fox limped slightly when he tried to come closer to sniff her but she imagined it was more from the awkwardness of the bandage than anything. He gave it a little shake as though he were trying to loosen it and, summoning her courage, she leaned down to give him a reassuring pet. By the time Petters had returned, carrying an additional cup of tea for Lillie and a handful of papers, the two of them had become fast friends.

"Thank you," she said, taking the cup from his hands. "You've got something." She nodded to the papers he was holding.

"Mm. Yes." Petters assumed his position on the wall and looped the leash around his wrist while the animal folded its back legs beneath himself and endeavoured to warm his hind end on the sun drenched ground. "It's interesting," he started, flicking through the papers and handing each one to Lillie after skimming them. "We've got an initial report of some mild skirmishes during the protest—looks like a fight broke out around three in the afternoon that day, whether or not it was related, I'm not sure. A few cuts and bruises reported. Nothing too earth shattering though."

Lillie perused the papers. "Anything else?" She looked closer at who the reporting officer was that day. "Hicks," she stated. "Is that the same Hicks who is recently deceased?" Petters peered over her shoulder to get a better look. "It is. He puts here he was called out to an incident that same evening at the King's Arms pub." Petters pointed to an initialed date and time stamp.

"But then nothing. Just that he was called out." Lillie scanned the report but there was no mention of anything else. No rape. No violence of any kind. Isn't that odd?"

"A little, yes. I would have thought he may have followed up. It's shoddy police work at the very least."

"Or something far worse," Lillie added. She looked up at her friend with trepidation. "Anything later on? In the following days or weeks?"

Felix handed her the entire stack of paper. "I've pulled all incident reports from the first of July through to the end of September but I don't see any other reference to any fallout from the march."

Lillie quickly flipped through the pages. There were reports on the theft of farm equipment, some mild skirmishes at various colleges, one report of an elderly woman claiming she had her purse stolen only to be followed up with another report that she had misplaced it. Lillie paused partway through and read in detail the report of a suicide of a young woman. "Do we know any more about this?" she asked, handing the report back to Felix while she continued her search.

Felix's eyes skimmed the paper. "Hanging. What a shame, and only twenty years old."

Finding nothing else about it in the other reports, she looked over Petters' shoulder. "Elsie Miller. What else does it say about her?"

Petters adjusted his glasses. "Found hanging in her parents' barn three miles outside of Oxford, August the second of 1921. Survived by three younger siblings. Was a student at the London School of Medicine and in her second year."

"Stop," Lillie ordered. "Can you repeat that?"

"It says here she was a student on summer break. The London School of Medicine."

"Like Adam Spool," Lillie said, slowly.

"Well, I'm sure their enrolment is quite high, it's a large school and being from Oxford it's a fairly easy commute. You can't necessarily assume they knew each other." Petters adjusted the leash on his wrist, the fox was standing again and pulling in order to get a better view of a couple of birds. "And anyway, the more vexing thing is that any witness I've got seems to be placing a woman at the scene of our crimes. Outside the pub, leaving the boat club after midnight, asking for Hicks at the police station right before he disappeared. I can't help but deduce that while Adam Spool might be strange and have some psychological issues, he isn't who we are looking for."

"But the parents acted so strangely, Felix. If you were there you would have suspected something—"

"I'm not dismissing it, Lillie, and we must certainly be aware that something is rather odd there—but it could just be that their son is crackers and they know it. What you are reading as strange could simply be their general discomfort with the whole situation."

"Mm. Possibly. I wonder if that girl, the one who committed suicide, was at the rally?"

"I'll go round and ask. Assuming her family is still in the same location."

"Good. And I will follow up with Harry. Anything new on the murdered chap in the river from yesterday morning?"

"Another Oxford student, as we thought. Went missing when he went outside to fetch some crates—apparently he was setting up for the regatta with a bunch of mates. They went out to look for him when he didn't come back—I assume he was drunk—and they presumed that he had wandered off home. When his roommate got back to their rooms later that evening and didn't find him there they reported him as missing."

"It's unbelievable," Lillie said. "This many murders in a town this size in such a short amount of time."

"Yes, and a missing dean, which I've had no luck on either. I've barely slept. I've got a constant rotation of officers scouring each and every nook and cranny of this village. I've set up an entire contingent, complete with dogs and the best investigators, to find the man. The mayor is absolutely incensed that we haven't made a whit of headway and is now threatening our funding. It's like the man has just vanished into thin air. I half wondered if we should be dredging the river but it's such a long process and the odds are so slim—but we may have to start anyway, just to rule it out."

Lillie gave the sleeping fox a quick pat. "Oxford City Royal Regatta starts in two days time, Felix. I suggest we all go and keep our eyes peeled and our ears to the ground. Whatever this is, it has to do with rowing students and everyone will be in the same place at one time."

She stood up and headed back down the street and towards home.

46

LILLIE

The next day Superintendent Felix Petters had gathered everyone at Tynesmore for an afternoon meeting.

"I wanted to keep this out of the police station so thank you, Harry, for hosting us," he said briskly, removing his hat and glancing around Harry's spring-green drawing room and out the French doors to the fields.

It was a startling view for anyone at any time of the year, and even if they had all seen it before multiple times, it did little to diminish their awe now. The summer sun had parched the grass from a vivid green to a golden honey and Lillie felt as though they had all just emerged from a De Wint painting and entered into the splendour of upper-class living. Rumple circled the room with a silver tray of freshly mint-garnished drinks in crystal glasses.

"An El Draque for you, miss?" he said, bowing slightly so Lillie could get a better view of the glass.

"Also known as a mojito?" she queried. Seeing his confusion, she expanded, "Rum, lime juice and sugar?" She wanted to be very sure before she took any cocktail from Rumple that she knew what was in it first. His last few had been nearly undrinkable.

"Certainly not. It is the signature drink of an illustrious English explorer, Sir Francis Drake. I don't know why the Americans area always trying to appropriate nearly every-thing." Rumple seemed affronted at her suggestion. "I've added mint," he continued, as if that changed things.

"Yes, yes of course, I see that. Which makes it a mojito." She frowned. "And incidentally, it's Cuban, not American."

"My apologies, miss." Rumple floated on to Felix Petters, who waved him away, and then onto Harry, who helped himself.

"How'd things go for you in London, Harry?" Felix asked.

Harry swallowed and winced. "Adam Spool was indeed a student at the London School of Medicine but he left his studies over a year ago and hasn't returned."

"Was there any suggestion of why?" Lillie asked, tentatively taking a sip of her own drink and finding that Rumple's cocktail concoctions weren't improving.

"Mm. I couldn't find out a thing from the administrative office—something or other about privacy—." Harry flicked his hair back. "But I stayed and asked around a bit and eventually found a couple of gents he had studied with. Seems he was a bit of a strange bird."

"How so?" Felix asked,

"Well, for starters, he didn't really chum around with men, preferring the company of women instead. As you can imagine, there aren't many women studying at the London School of Medicine but there was one in particular who he seemed to get on quite well with. At least until she had some sort of accident and didn't return to school."

"Were you able to get a name?" Lillie was often impressed with the amount of information Harry could squeeze out of a person just by setting them at ease with his well-utilized charm.

"I did ask but then promptly forgot. Ellie, maybe? Or Leah? Or..." Harry glanced out the window as his herd of horses picked up a gallop and came thundering towards the house.

"Elsie?" Lillie prompted.

"Yes! That's it. Elsie. How did you know that?"

"I'll tell you in a minute." Lillie didn't want Harry to get sidetracked.

"Anyway, he and this Elsie were nearly inseparable. Went everywhere together. At one point they'd had some argument with one of the lab instructors because he wouldn't allow Elsie to be in an anatomy class where they were dissecting a male corpse and Spool lost his temper and physically attacked the poor man. He was put on probation for it and nearly expelled but apparently the school relented and kept him on. He was quite a good student otherwise. Exceptional, really, or so a few have said—but volatile and well, one described him as slightly mad."

"So she was his girlfriend?" Lillie asked.

"Seems so. He was quite smitten with her, apparently." Harry looked to Petters. "Incidentally, why the clandestine meeting here and not at the station?"

"I'm not sure who I can trust at the moment." Felix ran his hand over his hair. "Whenever I've tried to investigate anything surrounding Hicks's history on the force, I've come up against a number of roadblocks. Either incomplete files or the sudden amnesia of his fellow officers. The collective memory of those who were close to Hicks is startlingly void."

Harry set his glass down. "If one can't trust the Oxford police who can one trust?" He motioned to Rumple for another drink. "So what of this Elsie?" he asked Lillie.

"I'll let Felix fill us in on that one—."

"Right." Petters answered. "It seems that Elsie *was* present at the franchise equality rally and was found dead just days later of an apparent suicide at her parent's farm. This is according to her sister who I've just come from interviewing. I ran the names of our other university victims by her to see if Elsie might have had relations with any of them but if she did, the sister wasn't aware."

"Has anyone been able to confirm whether or not she was at the Kings Arms pub on the evening of the rally?"

"Unsure," Felix responded. "She didn't come home right after the rally so it's possible, but where she went exactly isn't known, at least not by her sister."

Harry piped up. "So we have a case of a girl who went to a rally and then killed herself. Could be related, or not."

"I think it all centres around the pub, Felix, not necessarily the rally. You had an officer who was quiet about a skirmish there. We've got Jeremy who made a note to himself to report on a rape but then never did. We've got a girl who was at the rally and then killed herself just days after. We've got three dead Oxford students, a dead pub owner and the said police officer has also been murdered—not to mention a missing dean. What if this is all a cover up around a rape that happened at the Kings Arms pub and someone is taking their revenge?" Lillie set her drink down.

Felix nodded. "A friend of hers. This woman everyone seems to keep seeing at the place of each murder."

"She could be anyone, really." Lillie frowned. "A friend from school..."

"Not many women at the London School of Medicine, I can tell you," Harry put in.

"From here, then?"

"Possibly," Felix answered.

"So forget Adam Spool," Harry started. "He doesn't fit the description."

"Afraid not," Felix agreed. "And I don't want to waste putting man power on him if we haven't really got anything to go on. But could you do me a favour, Harry?"

"So long as you don't ask me to drink another one of those." Harry motioned to the sterling tray of drinks that had been placed on the bar with a look of disgust, even though he had just consumed two of them. Rumple wasn't anywhere to be seen.

"Follow David Spool tomorrow if you can. Let's just see what he is up to. It's regatta day and while I know he isn't much a of a rowing fan, it is a city-wide event and I wouldn't be at all surprised if he put in an appearance."

"I do rather wonder if I shouldn't have been a detective myself, superintendent." He nodded to Felix's uniform. "And we all know who would covet that uniform."

Rumple glided into the room with an impeccable sense of timing and a fresh tray of drinks while Harry winked at them.

47

HARRY

A s per the directive they had been given the previous day by Superintendent Felix Petters, Harry and Rumple were following David Spool.

The Oxford student crossed the narrow street a hundred feet ahead of them and darted quickly to the left through the weekend open-air floral market.

"I don't suppose he's on the hunt for a bunch of peonies." Harry remarked to Rumple who was making great swishing sounds behind him with his voluminous pantaloons. He'd taken to wearing them quite regularly after their trip to the cheating academic's lair, claiming they were more comfortable than the regular livery Harry provided. Harry had argued that Rumple never actually *wore* the livery he provided so how would he even know? Regardless, they really should have chosen something more befitting the clandestine operation they were on now. What *were* they thinking? "Can't you hurry, or are those just completely the wrong clothes for the job at hand?"

"I hardly think after a working with an organization as pres-tigious as the Defence of the Realm I should be hindered by a little extra fabric—a German U-boat, possibly, but not these trousers." Rumple picked up his pace somewhat, as though to illustrate his point.

Spool was continuing at speed past the stalls with the occasional glance behind him, and Harry ducked behind a cheesemonger's counter to avoid being detected, the smell of a particularly ripe stilton filling his nostrils.

"You are being more obvious doing that," Rumple criticized, carrying on past Harry until he was nearly ten feet away from Spool. Only then did he let up and begin to browse an antiquarian book stall with some enthusiasm.

There was a small cafe to the rear of the last row of market stalls and Spool ducked into the doorway and disappeared.

"Now what?" Harry huffed, catching up with Rumple who was holding a leather-bound copy of Volume One of John Milton's *Paradise Lost*. "You must be joking, Rumple. If we want to shop I suggest we do so when we aren't searching for a murderer run rampant."

Harry removed the book from his manservant's clutches and placed it back on the stand.

The bookseller, a man who looked himself to have been around since Milton's time, frowned his disapproval. "It's a second edition!" he called aggrievedly to their retreating backs.

Harry and Rumple entered the cafe and took a small table near the window with a good view of the front door and the kitchen entryway. Spool had situated himself at a table near the rear exit with his back to the two of them.

"I don't suppose he's having breakfast for one, do you?" Harry said, quietly.

Rumple remained silent, watching the Oxford student with some interest.

They waited for nearly twenty minutes, with Harry ordering coffee, toast and marmalade for the two of them while

Spool, on the other hand, had nothing. Every time the server circled his table he waved her away.

"Presumably he doesn't want to be stuck with a bill if he has to high tail it out of here," Harry surmised, hearing the chime of bells announcing a new customer and glancing towards the front door. "Well, would you look at that." He gave a long, low whistle under his breath as he watched a towering woman, with poker straight hair that hung like a sheet of rain, enter the cafe and take a seat across from David Spool.

"Eerie resemblance to the woman Petters painted a description of," Rumple agreed.

David Spool and his guest were already in engaged in a fairly heated conversation, with little to be seen of the usual formalities one would normally witness among acquaintances. The woman flipped back her hair in annoyance at something Spool said and lifted her bag off the floor as though she was planning on leaving. Spool then reluctantly reached into his pocket and retrieved a small bundle of bills, pushing them across the table where they disappeared within seconds into the bag.

"Why do you suppose an Oxford student is paying off the suspect of a murder investigation?" Harry whispered.

The woman stood to leave, then did the oddest thing. She turned, as though there was someone beside her, and blurted out a few sentences they couldn't decipher from where they sat.

"She's addressing the empty air beside her. How odd." Harry looked to Rumple to see if he'd noticed.

"Sir," Rumple urged. "She's leaving."

They waited nonchalantly as the woman in the coral dress hurried from the cafe using the back door while David Spool similarly exited past them, using the front door.

Harry and Rumple stood, placed what Harry hoped was enough money for the toast and coffee, and exited after the woman.

48

LILLIE

The shoreline of the Isis was littered with people. In addition to the crowds on the grass, a convoy of nearly sixty wooden rowboats lined the edge of the river and were filled with men and women in their summer best—striped blazers and straw hats, white lace dresses complete with parasols and picnic baskets—all hoping to get an even better view of the regatta than was visible from shore. The wealthier set, preferring land to the pandemonium on the water, had had their servants erect small duck-cloth tents on the grass at dawn and now their genteel families were easily seated on teak folding chairs sipping mint juleps and carbonated lemonades while the children searched for four-leaved clovers in the short grass.

The teams had been divided into heats and the early sets were warming up in the sunshine of the late morning, shifting their boats easily to the middle of the water and then slicing through it like a cluster of eels, their paddles dripping, turning, and reflecting off the water with each stroke.

"You'd never know this was a town with a killer on the loose, would you?" Lillie said, gazing up at Christ Church

Boat Club barge and its excessive bunting. The breeze caught the flags just as she said it, rippling their festive colours as if to make her point. "It's as though each barge is in competition over who can drape the most decoration across their facades."

Felix nodded his agreement. "It does feel as though the whole event is in denial of everything. Not to mention their main speaker is missing and we've still got nothing on the dean. It's as though he's just vanished into thin air."

"His wife must be beside herself," Lillie agreed, watching a small team of police officers as they moved from tent to tent, nodding their curt hello's. Lillie knew there were at least six teams that had been dispatched to the regatta, all with strict orders to search every square inch of the event without alarming the crowds. Felix himself had chosen plain clothes for the day, trading his wool uniform for a creamy blazer and tan trousers. A small straw fedora shielded his scalp from the sun. It was a calculated move on his part, not wanting to stand out in a crowd of spectators. If they were going to observe anything unusual at the regatta, chances were they would have better luck without the police reference.

"The dean is due to give the opening speech at noon. What do you suppose they plan to do about that?"

"Presumably they will just substitute in some city official, but it wouldn't hurt to be paying attention to the stage at that time." A crowd of already intoxicated young men pushed past them, laughing and Felix scowled his disapproval at their behaviour. "Is this what we have to look forward to with our youth?"

Lillie ignored him as they carried on past the other barges, all heavily weighted with newly-constructed bleachers that were fast filling up—some clubs had even hired musicians to entertain their guests while they watched the teams warm up.

"It is quite a spectacle, to say the least. And I thought Ascot was the height of the sporting season." Lillie grimaced her irritation with the clashing notes of the competing musicians.

Felix nodded. "This one is more accessible to your everyday man. It's like this every year, although I don't always make it. Jeremiah is here somewhere with a friend's family. You'd think the headless corpse at the Henley Regatta earlier in the season might have turned him off the whole idea of regattas, but apparently not."

"I think we should split up, Felix. Why don't I take all the area downstream from here and you go up."

Felix signalled his agreement. "You better make sure to do a run through of all the Oxford University barges.There's a lot of people, Lillie. It'll take some time."

"Go," she urged. "Meet you back here on the hour."

The two of them parted and Lillie hoped Harry was having better luck with David Spool. They needed a break and neither she nor Felix seemed to be in the right place to get it.

49

"You mustn't worry about things. They didn't see us, well...not the real us, anyway. By the time they put it all together we will be long gone."

She gave a look to suggest she wasn't buying it, her hazel eyes roaming around the boat shed in which they stood. Slivers of sunshine crept through the cracks in the walls and illuminated her hair, turning it from cinnamon to copper. She looked as beautiful as she always had—even the shadow around her neck had begun to pale. She motioned with one arm to the noise outside.

"Yes." It wasn't as though they didn't agree and they both knew how antsy she got with crowds. It wasn't any wonder after what she'd been through. "Listen, it's the grand finale. Once this is all neatly tied up we can move on from here. You always wanted to see New York, didn't you?"

Crowds, she repeated with a smirk.

Her perceptiveness was uncanny. As was her humour.

"Long Island, then. Cheer up."

The man writhed on the floor beneath them, covered now in the dirt from the shed. They'd nearly forgotten he was there.

The gag on his mouth had begun to come loose and they leaned down to fix it, giving him a firm nudge to remain quiet. His wrists were bleeding from the ropes but that was the least of their concerns.

They'll be here somewhere, she argued, again—referring to the police superintendent and the reporter. *Not to mention that entitled Plantagenet and his butler.*

"Yes, along with thousands of other people. If we even see them, we'll be gone before they can do anything."

They'd brought everything they needed and they lifted the metal gasoline can and placed it near the shell on the floor.

"Give me a hand with him, would you?" They tipped the shell slightly and managed to roll the body into it with some effort while the man squirmed. It was a older practice model but it would serve their purposes well enough. The shed was a little further up river from the Christ Church barge and wasn't used for much more than off-season storage for the university teams' gear. It made a suitable launching point and kept them out of sight until it was time.

They glanced at the wig and the coral dress, both of which lay heaped on the dirt floor beside the dean.

Shame, she lamented. *It was such a pretty dress.* She raised her eyes to the scene before them. The dean, bound and tied in an Oxford shell, ready to be set off down the river drenched in gasoline and lit on fire.

He wasn't really responsible, you know.

"Oh, he certainly was. He covered it all up and allowed those three to remain at university. They got to *go on* with their lives while their actions that night in the pub ended yours." The anger rose. "They took everything from us and he enabled it all because he didn't want his precious university to have its reputation soiled."

The dean gave a muffled protest from the floor of the shell.

"It's time." They could discuss it forever but ultimately the rape that had happened all that time ago, in that pub while the policed turned a blind eye and the pub manager pretended he didn't hear it, left them where they were today. In this shed on the edge of the Isis river, ready to put things right.

They doused the shell with gasoline while the dean futilely writhed and fought to scream. Then they dragged the entire stinking mess towards the rickety doors and the river beyond.

50

LILLIE

I t was nearly noon and still Lillie and Superintendent
Petters hadn't seen or heard anything out of the ordinary.
Most of the warm-up heats had finished and those teams
that were up first for racing were idly floating in the water
while their rowers received some last-minute coaching.

Harry caught up with them in the tented market stalls as
Petters was buying a couple of lemonades while they waited for
the opening speeches to start.

"You aren't going to believe this," he started, as Felix handed
Lillie her drink.

She took a long thirsty sip and wiped at her brow. "Go on."

"We followed David Spool as you suggested."

"Yes?" Lillie urged.

"Have you ever attended the weekend market? It's horribly
crowded, and the heat isn't doing anything beneficial for the
poor cheesemonger."

"Harry!" Lillie snapped. "Out with it; we really haven't much
time."

"Yes, yes of course. Well, Spool—he ended up in a cafe
outside the weekend market and there he met with a woman

meeting your description, superintendent. With just the hair you've described—it's like a curtain—and they had quite a heated exchange about something-or-other. Then Spool handed the woman a wad of bills, quite a large sum by the look of it if the handful was anything to go by."

"Where does a student like Spool get that kind of money?" Lillie asked, to no one in particular.

"I've no idea, but that isn't really the pivotal point here," Harry said.

"Oh?"

"Something was off, not right," Harry continued.

"I should think so, considering you are describing a woman we have now placed at the scene of not only the publican's murder, but also that of one of my officers." Petters frowned.

"Correct. And she was meeting with David Spool, the man who not only gave us cause to believe Edwin Hastock was murdered because he'd driven his car into the river with Flora Stewart and was receiving annual hate letters, but also was heading up the Hanwell programme where his brother had been admitted."

"But how is that last part relevant to..."

"Let me finish," Harry said, cutting her off. "They concluded their meeting and the woman headed out of the cafe and back through the market. While I followed, I had Rumple circle around and stage an intervention on her front side—really quite ingenious, the man belongs on the stage and not in my drawing room." Harry motioned for another lemonade from the freckled-faced boy at the stand while he plopped a few coins in the jar. "He feigned some sort of massive seizure and the woman had no choice but to stop walking as he was convulsing right in front of her. He rolled into her with some force, knocking her clear off her feet and voila!"

"Voila what, Harry?"

"*She*, my dear, is a *he*."

Lillie choked on her lemonade. "Are you saying—?" she sputtered.

"David Spool was meeting with his brother, yes."

"Adam Spool," Petters confirmed.

"Without the wig they look very similar, even with the makeup and skirt—the coral was really quite fetching, even Rumple thought it a very good choice. Unfortunately once the wig came off he was quite put out and he sprinted away from us so quickly that we lost sight of him. Admittedly I could be in better shape." Harry took a long gulp of lemonade and made a face. "Needs a little whiskey added," he called to the teenage boy manning the stand.

"So all this time we've been looking for a woman," Felix said, rubbing his forehead. "When it's a man—which makes sense, really. How else could she physically manage to drag these bodies here and there without help? It's stumped me."

"Adam Spool knew Elsie. We've confirmed that. I fully believe it was her who was raped after the equal franchise rally," Lillie started. "And then the poor girl killed herself."

"Hm. Yes. And my officer did nothing, hence the removal of his eyes. It's revenge, pure and simple. Adam Spool was in love with Elsie and when her life came to a tragic end, he snapped."

"And the publican heard the rape but also did nothing. So he removed his ears." Lillie felt sick.

"Well, given the body part the last murdered rower had removed, I think we can easily ascertain his role in the matter." Harry drained the last of his lemonade.

"I suppose Edwin Hastock and Andrew Blake were there and egging him on. Disgusting," Lillie added.

"I wouldn't doubt that Jeremy was ordered not to print by my very own officer," Petters concluded.

"It would have had to have been a very forceful directive in order to stop Jeremy Winston doing anything. And the dean? I suppose he covered up his students' roles in the whole matter."

Lillie gathered up her bag. "Regardless of his horrible behaviour, we need to find him and hope he is still alive."

The three of them moved away from the lemonade stand and into the sunshine. A quartet had started a festive tune on the boardwalk beside the water and on the air was a general feeling of summer enthusiasm and abandon.

"One does love a sporting event." Harry tipped his hat to shield his face. "Where is Rumple? I asked him to meet me here after parking the car, but I've seen nothing of him since and it's been at least a quarter of an hour."

"Do you see that?" Lillie pointed up the river to a man in the distance. He was dragging what appeared to be a fully loaded and very heavy shell towards the shoreline of the river.

Petters followed her line of vision but it was a few hundred feet away and even the sharpest eyes would have difficulty making it out.

"Ridiculous to load the bloody thing and then launch it." Harry fanned at his face. "What on earth has he got in there?" They all peered through the afternoon haze to better discern what they were looking at while Harry continued. "I once knew a chap on the practice squad who used to store his beer in an extra rowboat that he would launch alongside the team boats and then anchor it, tying the bottles to the rear of the boat and tossing them into the water to keep them cool—quite a bit of effort, now that I think of it, considering there was a pub a few hundred feet away." Harry held up his hand to shade his eyes. "Say, isn't that—?"

Lillie began to push her way through the crowds with Petters on her heels. "It's him, Felix...it has to be."

"I admit there is a resemblance...even from this distance," Harry answered.

"Let's go," Petters agreed.

Lillie broke into a run, dodging the dense clusters of people who had now gathered for the start, leaving the grandstands and spilling out of their tents to get closer to the water. There was a speaker on the main dock who was getting ready to launch the first race, the dean conspicuously absent in the chain of events. The man held up his trumpet and cleared his throat, putting his lips to the base and straining his voice to be heard above the general din, *Ladies and Gentlemen, I am proud to announce the start of the Oxford City Royal Regatta...*

"He's got something with him there, do you see?" Harry huffed behind them.

In the distance Lillie could see the tall man struggling with the weight of the boat, he held a metal can in one hand and was trying to drag the shell with the other, cursing as he hit a patch of long wet grass that slowed his process. He put the can down and used both hands to heave the boat off the grass and towards the river, then he picked up the can and placed it on top of whatever he had already loaded into the shell— muttering to himself as he did so. He looked up at one point, as though to survey his surroundings, said something to the air around him, then continued.

"Be careful, Lillie," Petters called to her. "We are dealing with someone who is visibly insane."

Adam Spool had yet to see them, so intent was he on the job at hand. He reached the water's edge just as the gun went off behind them, announcing the start of the first heat, and the simultaneous roar of the crowds deafened their own interchange. Lillie knew Harry was saying something to her but she couldn't hear a thing past the pulsing in her veins as her legs continued to pound like pistons towards Spool and the loaded shell.

They were within thirty feet of him when he pushed the shell into the water and reached into his pocket for something. Lillie smelled the gasoline just a split second before she saw Spool light a soaked rag on fire and toss it into the floating shell as it moved away from him down the river, causing the front of the boat to burst into flames. By the time she flung herself into the river behind the boat it was nearly out of reach. She could hear the splash of water behind her as Harry did the same and she broke into front crawl confident that he was near enough to her to help. Gulping and gasping for air she managed to catch the boat just as she saw Rumple ten feet ahead of her on the shore of the river. He too, flung himself into the water and began swimming towards the boat which was now nearly engulfed in flames. The three of them, realizing the bound body on the floor of the boat was not only alive but struggling, managed to capsize the entire thing forward and tip the dean into the water where he was caught by Rumple who had circled around in order to catch him. In a flurry of excess fabric ballooning around them, the bound dean and Rumple managed to get to shore where a small crowd had realized what was going on and had come to help pull them from the water.

By the time Lillie and Harry had made it out of the water themselves, Felix had managed to tackle Adam Spool and had him sitting in handcuffs on the muddy edge of the river. Spool was muttering something incoherent to no one in particular.

Lillie dragged herself and her sopping dress over to Felix.

"Impressive, young lady." He smiled at the mess before him. "Where did you learn to swim like that?"

"I had a crush on a boy at the local pool," she said, wiping a stray piece of weed from her face and flinging it to the ground. She looked over at Adam Spool and was overcome with sudden empathy for him. "I hope he will get the help he needs, Felix. He's insane, jail isn't where he belongs."

"I'll do my best, Lillie. And I agree with you."

Harry had wandered over to them, along with a couple of the officers who Felix had tasked with circling the event. The officers lifted Spool up off the grass by his forearms and escorted him towards the parked police cars.

"Looks like you got your man," Harry said, flipping his wet

hair off his forehead and watching them go. "Or should I say woman?" Even drenched, Harry still looked as though he belonged in the finest London restaurant.

"Seems so, how is the dean?" Petters asked.

"Somewhat traumatized and a few burns on his legs but otherwise very lucky." Harry looked at Lillie and frowned. "Did that chap at the pool teach you nothing all those years ago? A little more extension on that left arm, Lillie, how many times must I tell you? You'd go a lot faster."

DANIEL

It was early and Oxford train station was exceptionally quiet. Sundays usually were, Daniel thought to himself, as he watched an old man sweep yesterday's refuse into a small bucket and then dispose of it into a larger bin on his wooden rolling cart. He gave him and Lillie an almost imperceptible nod as he passed by and headed to the far end of the platform, the wheels on his cart squeaking and groaning as he moved, protesting their early shift.

Neither of them had slept much, Daniel's imminent departure on both of their minds as they had made love through the night—at first softly and gently and then more urgently as the dawn broke. It was as though they needed to stamp themselves with some memory of their last night together. When they finally had slept, Lillie had found herself waking throughout the night and reaching for his hand, seeking it as she would water in a desert, as though her lips and throat were parched from wanting, as were his. No time together was ever enough.

She remained silent, probably knowing there wasn't anything she could say now to stop him going and fearful if she did speak her voice would waver. He looked down at her, his grey eyes steely and hard as though if he made them so he could somehow summon the courage to leave her, but it was futile.

He turned towards her abruptly and folded her into his long arms, pulling her in and breathing into her hair. "As soon as it's sorted I'll come for you," he whispered, as though it would make a difference now.

How could he possibly? He was going back to America and they had no idea when or if he could return. What if they killed him? she'd argued immediately after he'd told her of his plan to leave. I won't let them, he'd argued back and she'd had to concede that whoever was coming for him likely wouldn't stop until he either went back and made amends or...he shuddered, trying not to imagine all the scenarios and grateful Lillie couldn't either. Daniel would have to kill them, it was that simple. That was the world he'd created for himself and the world he was now trying to escape. But could he ever really escape the dark underworld of criminality? And Lillie knew all about the mobs in America and their connections to Europe. Italian immigrants, Jewish immigrants, Irish immigrants—all carving out a piece of America to fit their economic agendas— the streets of New York and Boston and Chicago their battle-grounds. They were ruthless.

He pulled back and looked into her eyes. For the moment he wished he could swallow her. "You'll need to keep them with you," he said, referring to the security personnel he'd hired for her cottage and she nodded to keep him satisfied. "Even that may not be enough." He hardened his mouth. "You'll have to forgive me."

"What for?" she asked, confused at what he was referring to.

He avoided her gaze, knowing it would make her uneasy.

"Daniel," she insisted again. "What for?"

He opened his mouth as though to speak, then shut it again,

considering. When he finally looked at her, the expectant look on her face encouraged him to give her something, even though it wasn't nearly everything she wanted to hear.

"For making sure you and Lola are in the best, most capable hands possible," he said finally. It was evasive, of course it was.

She gave him a look that said she wanted the rest of the explanation, but what could he possibly say that wouldn't make her fly off the platform in a rage? He'd taken measures. Extreme measures, personal measures—to make absolutely sure she had not only security, but also someone who was used to dealing with underworld figures. Someone who was legitimate and could harness the entire national intelligence resource pool if he had to in order to protect the woman Daniel loved. Not only that, the personal connection ensured Lillie would be the highest priority. He hadn't had any choice in the matter. The solution had been as clear as day for him.

They were interrupted by the whistle of the London train, heaving its great black bulk to the platform in a cloud of steam and screeching metal. Daniel instantly felt the anxiety rise in his chest. He was going and he was so hopelessly in love with her. They watched as the passengers unloaded and the porters hurried forward to whisk away their cases while she swallowed back her tears.

A familiar face came towards them out of the haze from the train. The walk, the stature, the dark hair—Lillie had to blink in order to make sure she was seeing correctly. The man headed towards them as though they were exactly who he had just travelled from London to see. She must have thought it was just an uncomfortable coincidence.

Daniel hesitated briefly, and then stepped forward to greet him. Would Lillie think he was going to disappear? Or shield her from the man? Instead, and to her obvious surprise, he reached out one long arm and shook the man's hand.

Daniel heard her breath catch in her throat and he longed

to turn to her and explain somehow. Everything was happening so fast and he'd said nothing to her.

"Thanks for coming, Jack," Daniel said to the man who had once been Lillie's fiancé.

"Of course." Jack replied, and Daniel felt an irrational jealously surge through his veins. "I can take things from here. You needn't worry." He said it with such smoothness and confidence that despite his feelings, Daniel knew he'd made the right choice.

Jack looked past him and smiled at Lillie, his blue eyes boring a hole through her startled ones. She looked as though her whole world had just given way.

"Hello, Lillie," he said, as though it were the most natural thing in the world.

ALSO BY LISA ZUMPANO

An Unfortunate End

A Willful Grievance

A Fine Duplicity

A Secret Agenda

All The Pieces

Made in the USA
Columbia, SC
20 November 2021